ULTIMATE AUTOGRAPH HUNTERS

RUTH MASTERS

Ultimate Autograph Hunters
by Ruth Masters

First published 2022. This version published 2023

© Ruth Masters

ISBN: 9798853339835
Imprint: Independently published

The right of Ruth Masters to be identified as the author of this work has been asserted by her in accordance with the Copyright, Designs and Patents Act 1988.

All rights reserved. No part of this publication may be reproduced, stored in or introduced into a retrieval system, or transmitted, in any form, or by any means (electronic, mechanical, photocopying, recording or otherwise) without the prior written permission of the publisher. Any person who does any unauthorised act in relation to this publication may be liable to criminal prosecution and civil claims for damages.

Cover by The Planet Zarg Design Studio. "TP" designed by Robert Hammond.

This book is sold subject to the condition that it shall not, by way of trade or otherwise, be lent, re-sold, hired out, or otherwise circulated without the publisher's prior consent in any form of binding or cover other than that in which it is published and without a similar condition including this condition being imposed on the subsequent purchaser.

Books by Ruth Masters

Truxxe
All Aliens Like Burgers
Do Aliens Read Sci-Fi?
When Aliens Play Trumps
The Complete Truxxe Trilogy Special Edition

Zealcon
The Extreme Autograph Hunters
The Ultimate Autograph Hunters

Möbius
Belisha Beacon & Tabitha Turner

Order from www.ruthmastersscifi.com

PROLOGUE

Rosemary Yates was on her way to ZealCon, the biggest science fiction and fantasy event in the Midlands.

She had passed her driving test almost three months ago, but this was the first proper road trip she had taken in her silver Suzuki Swift. Of course, it wouldn't be a proper road trip if she were to travel alone; she needed a travelling companion. And as her friend Joanne Harrison's house was practically en-route to the convention, it made sense for the two of them to travel together. Rosemary just had to negotiate the M1 first. As she travelled along the highway, she wished that she had not opted to drive in flip-flops for they did not help to make the most comfortable journey. Of course, once they arrived at the event, the two of them would be walking around barefoot, like the faerie characters that they would be portraying on the first night of the convention.

She closed the window for it was too draughty – particularly as she was only wearing a thin, handmade faerie costume and her coat was in the boot with the rest of her luggage.

I hope I'm not involved in an accident, she thought. *I don't fancy being dragged out of my car wearing this. Perhaps I should have got changed when I got there. I doubt anyone else will be travelling in full costume.*

Rosemary turned on the radio to block out her worries and began to sing along to a song that reminded her of her teenage years. Next, the radio DJ played a song which reminded her of last year's ZealCon. She grinned as she remembered jumping around the dance floor in the early hours with Joanne and lots of other people she had met that weekend. It was such a fun event. It was one of the few places that she could really be herself, not worry about what anyone else thought and just enjoy the moment. The weekend always went so quickly though, and the waiting time between events was often painfully slow, but it was always worth the wait. Rosemary had painstakingly made her costume from scratch and had spent the last few weeks consulting books of faerie lore, perusing fabric shops and being hunched over her sewing machine. She had been comparing notes with Joanne, who had been working on her own attire, the idea being that the girls' costumes complemented each other. Joanne was definitely the more creative of the two. She enjoyed the whole costume-making process, but Rosemary merely found it a means to an end; the fun part for her was actually wearing the finished result. Both girls were looking forward to the Faerie Gathering, an unofficial annual meet-up of like-minded people which traditionally took place on the Saturday evening of the event. The Gathering had been where the girls had met.

The girls were not just fans of the fantasy genre, however. For example, they had discovered at ZealCon two years previously that they were both quite intrigued about a long-running science fiction series called *Sir Cuthbert's Remarkable Adventures Through Time*. On discovering this new programme (or new to them, at least), they had got together and binge-watched every single episode over the course of a fortnight during the summer, interspersed with conversations on ideas for costumes and discussions over the programme in beer gardens. Rosemary had quickly become fascinated by the bespectacled intellectual who travelled through time in his tepee-shaped metallic steam-punk Temporal Perambulator (or TP for short). His adventures were full of colourful characters, extraordinary scenarios and stunning backdrops. How Rosemary would love to travel with Sir Cuthbert!

And eleven series later, the programme was just as compelling to watch. Rosemary obeyed her Sat Nav (even though it took her the long way around Joanne's housing estate) and eventually pulled up at number seven, Oak Tree Crescent. She was about to get out of the car for a leg-stretch when the front door of number seven opened and out bounded Joanne. Grinning with excitement, she handed Rosemary her handbag, bounced back up the driveway and emerged a few moments later with a bulging suitcase. Rosemary opened the boot so that Joanne could stow the case inside with one almighty heave, then gave her friend a hug.

"It's about time!" Joanne exclaimed. I've been waiting by the door like an excited puppy all morning.

"I never would have guessed!" laughed Rosemary.

Joanne did up her seatbelt, checked her appearance in the mirror on the inside of the sun visor and turned to her friend.

"Road trip!" she shouted with glee and made a fist with her hand which she pumped a few times in the air.

"Oh yes. I can't wait!" Rosemary joined in with the fist-pumping.

They had barely got to the other end of the crescent and Joanne was already chatting away – finally able to speak to her friend in person.

"Oh, and have you heard?"

"Heard what?" asked Rosemary as she checked her rear-view mirror and pulled onto the main road.

"About the special announcement!" Joanne squealed with delight.

"What special announcement?"

"I thought – out of the pair of us – that you would know about it first. ZealCon announced it in the last hour. Well, you were probably driving. So ... have a guess."

"OK. Is it a special guest?"

"Kind of," said Joanne, teasingly. "Think of a character that's been there from the beginning. Well, from the beginning of a certain TV show anyway."

"Sir Cuthbert ... Mathias Price?"

"Almost ..."

"Er ... I don't know." Rosemary shrugged and her focus remained on the road ahead.

"OK, so it's not a character exactly, more of a prop ..."

"The ... the TP?" asked Rosemary, hopefully.

She saw Joanne's head of curls nodding in the edge of her vision.

"Yep. The latest one, from the new series. Series 12."

"Ooh, I don't even know what that one looks like."

"You do *have* the internet at home, don't you?"

"You know I do!" Rosemary protested. "I just don't like spoilers, that's all."

"Well, I think even you can make an exception in this case," said Joanne. "Isn't it exciting though? All these guest announcements, the parties, the Faerie Gathering, the stalls selling all the shiny merchandise and now this ... we *have* to get a photograph with it."

"I wish I'd packed one of my costumes from *Sir Cuthbert* now," sighed Rosemary.

"It doesn't matter – I've got a few with me if you want to borrow one. I bet you'd look amazing as Kalisa Clarke from 'The Woman with the Silver Locket' – I'm too pasty and blonde to pull off that character anyway. She's fabulous. There are some great costumes in that story aren't there? Your outfit looks fantastic by the way! I'm glad you went with that material rather than that flimsy chiffon stuff. Did you have much trouble finding all the sequins and flowers? Oh, and how do you manage to drive in flip-flops? I don't think that I could. And by the way ..."

Rosemary let her excitable friend witter away as she concentrated on the journey. She smiled to herself as they got nearer and nearer to the venue. She couldn't wait for the weekend to begin.

They had checked into the hotel with ease. Although the queue had been rather long, it had been fun talking to other attendees in the queue and comparing costumes and itineraries for the weekend ahead. Now Joanne was making a big deal out of unpacking and hanging her costumes, filing them in the hotel-room wardrobe according to television programme and genre and lining up her shoes.

"You do know that this is only a weekend-long event, don't you?" Rosemary teased her.

"I know. But it's nice to have the choice, isn't it? Have you brought a hairdryer with you? I didn't have any room in my case for mine."

"There's one in here," said Rosemary. She opened one of the drawers in the dressing table and disclosed a hairdryer and Bible. "Hotel-room staples," she informed her with a shrug.

"As are these!" Joanne pointed to a pile of miniature toiletries which she had swiped from the en-suite bathroom on arrival. "You can have the ones that housekeeping leave us tomorrow."

"If you like," said Rosemary with a laugh. "As long as I can have the bath towel."

Joanne stopped and stood still, open-mouthed.

"I was joking!"

The two of them laughed.

"Anyway, once we're both ready, shall we make our way down to the bar?" Joanne suggested.

"Of course."

The bar was thronged with convention goers; people dressed smartly, people in costume, people in geeky t-shirts, people who had evidently arrived straight from work, people their age, older people, teenagers ... But they all had one thing in common; they were all excited to be there. The atmosphere was tangible. Joanne turned to Rosemary and grinned.

I've been looking forward to this for so long!" she enthused. "I can't believe we're finally back here – here at the Ballington Hotel – our second home."

The girls shared a plate of nachos in the busy bar area of the hotel. Joanne dipped three at once into the huge dollop of guacamole.

"The Ballington Hotel is the best place to get these you know," said Rosemary. "Nowhere else seems to get the nacho-to-topping ratio right," she clarified. Joanne gave her a thumbs-up by way of agreement and crunched her way through a mouthful.

"So, what's the plan for tomorrow?" Joanne rubbed her hands together to free them from crumbs and opened the new, pristine copy of the 2012 ZealCon programme. "It looks like things kick off quite early with panels and photoshoots from 9am."

Rosemary turned the programme so that it was facing her and quickly scanned through the glossy pages.

"I'd like to meet James L. Robertson, Sir Cuthbert's stunt double," she said.

"Well, that's a given."

"So that's one panel, one autograph session and photograph session to start off with. Plus, William Shatner."

"Of course," the girls said in unison. "And, no doubt, his queue will be huge ... so maybe we should get up early and queue up for his autograph and then go to the James L. Robertson panel and then ..."

"What does the programme say about the TP? Are there official photo sessions for that or can we just use our phones as and when? It didn't say on the website." Joanne grabbed another handful of nachos and let her friend thumb through the, currently, unspoiled booklet.

"Hmm, I'm not sure. I think it was supposed to be a surprise until the last minute, so maybe it's not in here." Rosemary gave a shrug.

"Are you talking about the Temporal Perambulator?" A girl appeared at the table. She was petite, with cropped, bright-red hair in which she wore a yellow flower. She was dressed in a floaty, lilac many-layered dress and wore no shoes. She was evidently there for the Faerie Gathering also. "I was talking to those guys over there in the check-in queue this afternoon about what it said on the forum about it being the Series 12 TP. Do you see the one dressed as Sir Cuthbert and his friend? Anyway, it's quite exciting, eh?" The girl took it upon herself to grab a nearby vacant stool, drag it to the table and promptly join them. "May I?" she asked, pointing to the sharing dish.

Joanne shrugged and the girl helped herself to a nacho. She dipped it into a dollop of sour cream and continued.

"They're due to start filming Series 12 in April, so it's a bit of publicity I suppose. Hey, were you two here at last year's event?"

"Yes. I'm Joanne by the way and this is Rosemary."

"Of course! I can recognise that fantastic needlework anywhere – such impressive costumes! I remember you two now. I'm Lottie. We were all dancing with those Stormtroopers with their helmets off until about 4am and then we were chatting in the bar, debating which is the best sewing machine, do you remember?"

"Yes, I remember!" Rosemary gave a laugh in sudden recollection. "Lottie. Oh yeah!"

"I had blue hair last time, of course. That was a great night, wasn't it?"

"I still cringe about my dance-floor air guitar," said Rosemary, covering her eyes. "I really thought I was a rock star or something that night!"

"I remember that!" Lottie grinned. "Good times. I'm really excited about this event. I love the Faerie Gathering too – everyone is just so nice; no one in that group criticises your costume, no one judges. It's just a nice group to be a part of, isn't it?"

"It's a rarity these days," admitted Joanne. "The Gathering is certainly a little oasis of calm. OK ... not calm ... contentment. Happiness. Well ... craziness – in a good way!"

"Exactly," agreed Lottie. "Anyway, I'd better go and find my roommate, Annabelle. I'll see you both tomorrow, yeah?"

"See you later," they said in unison. Lottie had barely stood up before her stool was dragged to another busy table by a girl dressed in an anime costume.

"I can't believe how many people are here this year. This place is packed!" Rosemary remarked. She glanced over at the bar which was three people deep. "Do you want a drink? Those green cocktails look interesting. And if you don't fancy one now, then you might by the time I get to the front of the queue!"

"Yes please," said Joanne, setting the empty plate aside. "I'll get the next one."

Having caught up with various people that they knew from previous events, Rosemary and Joanne decided to wander around and see if there was anyone new and interesting to talk to.

"Aren't those guys the ones that Lottie was talking about?" Joanne sucked on her curly straw and nodded in the direction of where she wanted Rosemary to look in a not-so-inconspicuous fashion.

"You mean that shy-looking dude and the drunk one with black paint smudged over his nose? Yeah, I think so."

"Let's go over and say hello." Joanne nudged her so hard that Rosemary almost spilled her drink down her dress. "They look like fun. And they're Sir Cuthbert fans."

Joanne, being Joanne, led the way through the crowded bar.

"Hey!" she called out, instantly gaining the attention of the two men. "Great costumes!"

"Why thank you, kind faerie," said the man with the polish-smeared face. He bowed low to the ground. The girls might have been impressed, if he hadn't wavered and stumbled on his way back up.

"Sir Cuthbert and er …" Joanne stammered.

"I think I know," said Rosemary. "Are you cosplaying that character from 'The Escape from Stevington Manor'? That street urchin?"

Alistair pretended to look aghast.

"*Street urchin*, dear faerie? I am *offended*!" he said, dramatically. Rosemary could not help but laugh. "I am, of course, the *young boot polisher*."

"That's a pretty obscure choice to make," said Joanne. "The role isn't even credited!"

"Which is a pity, as the character did have some lines," Jeremy chipped in. "Although they were cut in the final edit."

Rosemary was a fan of the television programme, but she admitted to feeling a little lost when the boot polisher and her friend began reeling off chunks of dialogue from the episode in question.

"I'm Jeremy," the shy, Sir-Cuthbert-clad man introduced himself.

"Rosemary," she said and shook his hand.

Jeremy jabbed a thumb in the direction of his friend. "Alistair and I were considering sneaking in for a look at the TP before the hall actually opens," he said. "We were going to go and see if we could find it tonight."

"Seriously?" Rosemary took a few moments to process the information then leaned in closer. It was difficult to hear him speak against the hubbub. "But why?"

"Well, just so that we can be the first, really."

"I see," she took a sip of her cocktail and pondered. "And how are you planning to do that?"

"Well, it can't be that difficult, can it? It's not as though the thing would have bodyguards like the guests do, and I doubt that this model is made of gold. I'm assuming that it's going to be sitting in the main hall, ready for tomorrow."

"I suppose so. But what if the room is locked?"

"Well hopefully we can find a way." To her surprise, Jeremy asked, "Would you er … would you and Joanne like to come along with us? Only if you want to. You don't have to, of course. We could just er … Al and I could just take some pictures and show you tomorrow. Well by tomorrow you can see it for yourselves so you probably won't need to see the pictures so it would be a bit pointless but er …" Jeremy's face reddened slightly and he squinted, as though he felt incredibly uncomfortable – like he had asked for her hand in marriage and instantly regretted it.

Rosemary rested a hand on his shoulder in a bid to comfort the poor man.

"I would love to come along. Sounds like fun – a bit of adventure! And I'm sure that Jo will too. She's always up for a laugh."

"Come on, come on. Why do you always take so long to get ready?" complained Joanne. "If we don't hurry, the guys will have been and gone already and they'll have had their photographs taken before us!"

"Is this really about them getting their pictures before us?" asked Rosemary as she opened her makeup bag. She sought out her mascara and applied a fresh coat onto her already dark lashes. "Or are you keen to meet up with that boot polisher again? I saw how you looked at him."

"Well, he is kind of cute. In a geeky sort of way."

"And geeky is the *best* way."

"Exactly. Now, come *on*."

"All right, I'm nearly ready. Just wait one second while I go to the toilet."

As the door to the en suite closed, Joanne gave a silent scream of frustration. "And anyway, you can talk!" Joanne called through the door. "You seem to be going to a lot of trouble prettifying yourself before we meet up with them again. And Jeremy is *definitely* your type."

Rosemary didn't reply. A few moments later, Joanne heard the toilet flush, the running of water and then the door finally opened.

"Come on then," said Rosemary, grabbing her bag and key card. "Let's go to the Elizabeth Suite and find the new TP!"

The girls found the suite with little difficulty. There didn't seem to be any hotel staff around in that part of the hotel and the door had been left ajar.

"The lights are on. They must be here already," Rosemary whispered.

"They've probably been here ages. We're twenty minutes late!"

The girls scanned the room for any sign of the TP or the two young men. There was no sign of either. They looked at each other in confusion.

"This has to be the right place," said Rosemary. She wandered across to the other side of the room where she found a long table displaying various artefacts which related to *Sir Cuthbert's Remarkable Adventures Through Time*. There was a mock-up of Sir Cuthbert's diary, a porcelain figure of Sir Cuthbert and a miniature version of the Series 1 Temporal Perambulator among other paraphernalia. The most curious thing about the display was not the things upon it, but the large, inconspicuous space next to it.

"Jo!" she shouted. Her friend soon appeared at her side. "Do you suppose … it looks like this is where the TP is *going to be*. Perhaps they haven't brought it in yet."

"Well, that's disappointing." Joanne's shoulders fell. "After all the trouble we went to as well. You'd think that the boys would have waited for us anyway, or at least left us a note."

"They've probably gone off in a strop back to their room. They both seem the type."

"I think I'm going to do the same," sighed Joanne.

"Oh well. At least we'll see them tomorrow. And the TP."

But Rosemary could not have been more wrong. For the next day, the TP was still conspicuous by its absence and Alistair and Jeremy were nowhere to be found.

"I wish we'd got their phone numbers," said Rosemary as they joined the end of the line for a photoshoot with Warwick Davis. "Then we would at least know that they're OK."

"There are hundreds of people here, Rosie. I'm sure they're fine. They must be here somewhere or else sleeping off hangovers."

"You're right. Let's just get on with our itinerary, shall we? We could keep checking back to see whether the TP has arrived yet. The Faerie Gathering is after lunch so we can't miss that."

Rosemary and Joanne spent the morning queuing for photoshoots and autographs and meeting up with friends old and new. They were blissfully happy in the company of each other and in the familiar, amiable atmosphere of ZealCon. For the Faerie Gathering they were granted access to a quieter conference suite and enjoyed poring over beautifully illustrated books that collectors had bought along and discussing fantasy lore with like-minded fans of the genre. They sampled "lembas bread" made by a fan of *Lord of the Rings* and drank sweet tea which was served by a barefoot man in purple who wore the most beautiful pair of wings that they had ever seen. The Gathering's organiser showed film clips on a large plasma screen. At this point, Rosemary's bare feet were getting a little itchy.

"Shall we go and see if the TP is here yet?" she asked Joanne.

"We may as well. I remember this video from last year, anyway."

"Hey, where are you two going?" It was Lottie. She followed them as they ducked out of the conference room. "I can't believe you're cutting the Gathering short! I've waited all year for this."

"Then stay. Don't miss it on our account, Lottie. We're going to see if the TP is here yet."

"Oh, it should be," she said, flatly. "I saw them unloading it off a truck yesterday afternoon.

Rosemary and Joanne looked at each other.

"What?" gasped Joanne. "Then why isn't it here? We've searched every corner of the convention for it."

Lottie shrugged. "Well, I'll see you two later I guess. I want to stay until the end."

The pair nodded as Lottie went back in and closed the door behind her.

"How strange," said Rosemary. I'm going to go and talk to the woman who owns the stall with all the Sir Cuthbert items on it. She might know something."

The girls approached the stall and found a sombre-looking woman studying her phone. She was shaking her head in disbelief.

"Are you all right?" Joanne asked her.

"Haven't you heard?"

"Heard what?"

"I thought there had been an announcement or something. They were talking about cancelling the event until it was sorted."

"What?" Joanne asked.

"The set piece that I arranged to be brought here for a special appearance … the Series 12 TP. It's gone!"

"Gone? How could it have gone? Who would take it? No one here, surely. And *how*?"

"I … I can't get my head around it." The woman took a tissue from her sleeve and blew her nose. "I don't know what to do. I'm responsible for it while it's not on set. I don't know whether to stay here and carry on or pack up and go home and insist that the place gets cordoned off? It's a crime scene after all."

"When did it go missing?" asked Rosemary, puzzled.

"Well, it took three of us to set it up last night and the room was locked up at about nine o' clock. And this morning it was gone!"

Rosemary gulped. She stopped herself from blurting out that the room was open in the early hours of the morning and was glad that Joanne was keeping quiet about it too. Whatever had happened, she didn't want to get Jeremy and Alistair into trouble unnecessarily.

"Have they checked the CCTV footage?" asked Joanne, doubtfully.

"Yes." The woman nodded. "There is a camera pointing directly to the only door to the outside and it shows nothing. Just hours of footage of a door which is firmly shut. It doesn't make any sense. And it's far too big to get out of any of these." She waved an arm at both of the internal doors which led out of the large conference room.

"Does it fold up?" Rosemary asked.

"If it did, they wouldn't need to transport it on the back of a truck," said Joanne.

"Quite," said the woman. "And how did you know about the truck?"

"Oh, a friend told us she saw it yesterday. Incidentally – is the truck still here?"

"It's still in the car park, yes. So, whoever took it hasn't taken that too. But I … I don't want to go around accusing anyone. Oh, it doesn't make sense. It's so big and heavy and … impossible."

"I wish I knew what to do," said Rosemary. "I was looking forward to seeing the TP and I feel helpless."

"Me too," said Joanne, not taking her eyes off the weeping woman.

"Don't worry about me," she told them sincerely. "You two go off and enjoy the convention if they've decided not to cancel it after all. Just let me know if you hear anything, OK?"

"Of course."

Rosemary and Joanne went back to their room for lunch. They discussed their concerns about the missing TP while Rosemary showed off her culinary skills using a kettleful of boiling water and two sachets of noodles. They bounced ideas around from the prospect of someone at the convention being malevolent enough to actually steal the prop, to the outright absurd. As Rosemary handed a bowlful of hot, rehydrated carbohydrates to her friend, she told her what was on her mind. Joanne nearly dropped the steaming bowl in surprise.

"You and your imagination, Rosie! So, because the TP isn't here and we can't find the boys, your conclusion is that Jeremy and Alistair have stolen it and have embarked on a journey through time?"

"I can't think of another plausible explanation. Can you?"

I think you and I have different ideas of the meaning of the word *plausible*."

"So, what shall we do?"

"Well, there's not a lot we *can* do. Whatever's happened, I feel a bit helpless really. And that poor woman ..." Joanne blew on her noodles and sucked up a noisy forkful.

"Perhaps she's hidden it!" Rosemary suddenly gasped. "She *wants* everyone to think that something has happened to it, but really, it's all part of a prank and just as James L. Robertson is due to start his panel, it'll be wheeled onto the stage and he'll jump out of it!"

"It's possible, I suppose. Although it seems a little elaborate."

"You're probably right," sighed Rosemary. "And she did seem genuinely devastated."

Despite the disappearance of the legendary timemachine, the girls made the best of the weekend. They collected autographs in their matching black books, had photographs taken with some of their favourite celebrated stars and mingled with many interesting people. On the Sunday of the event, they decided to have another look at some of the items that they had been eyeing on the merchandise tables. Rosemary opted for a picture of the characters from *Farscape* which had been burned onto a piece of wood with a pyrography pen. It was an impressive piece and both girls agreed that the craftmanship and time that had gone into the work was astounding. It would look perfect on her mantelpiece. Joanne, however, had something quite different in mind and spent the last of her budget on the stall which belonged to the owner of the TP. She chose to purchase the mock-up of Sir Cuthbert's diary, which was very much like the one used in the programme. She marvelled at the quality of the product; a beautifully embossed leather-bound book containing detailed diary entries and little scribbled notes and doodles inside. Joanne was talking to the woman who owned the stall for quite some time and she had somehow talked her into buying something else from her – at a reduced cost (or so she had assured her). This second item was even more special than the first in Rosemary's view. It was another book, and this one contained the co-ordinates of all of the times and places that Sir Cuthbert had visited throughout history. To Rosemary's delight, it even included places and times that had not featured in the programme. Its author had evidently gone to a lot of trouble to produce it.

Rosemary expressed her opinion that this book held clues as to where the time traveller would visit in future episodes and pored over the book for most of the afternoon. When Joanne finally got her possession back from her friend, she argued that that was not necessarily the case and that the extra entries had been added simply to bulk out the book. Either way, the girls agreed that it was a stunning piece of memorabilia to own.

Sundays are known to be more subdued at such weekend-long events and ZealCon was no different. Most attendees were, although still elated, suffering from exhaustion, hangovers and empty pockets. By the evening, many people had left, although some people could still be found lingering in the bar, delaying their journey home and preparing for the inevitable post-con come-down. Rosemary and Joanne, however, were two of the few people who remained in the Elizabeth Suite, enjoying a mini-debrief of the weekend's events. The celebrity guests were either on their merry way home or relaxing in another part of the hotel, no doubt exhausted. As the last of the dealers packed away the remainder of their unsold wares and exited the double door which led to the loading bay, the girls suddenly found themselves alone in the hall.

"Where did everyone go?" asked Rosemary.

"We were so engrossed in our conversation that we didn't notice everyone leaving!" exclaimed Joanne and threw back her head in laughter. However, her laughter was soon drowned out by a familiar humming sound. A plume of smoke, bathed in green light, shot up towards the ceiling and quickly dispersed.

The Temporal Perambulator had appeared right in front of them.

"Blimey, Jimey!" exclaimed an extremely scruffy-looking Alistair. "That was one hell of a ride. Oh, hello again, ladies!" He bowed low and tumbled out of the Temporal Perambulator.

Jeremy stumbled after him, looking just as unkempt and fatigued.

"Don't *hello ladies* us," huffed Joanne. "You two have some explaining to do. I can't believe you went to the Elizabeth Suite without us. And you missed the entire convention." She crossed her arms across her chest and gave the air of an angry mother hen.

"I think you're missing something more important here—" Rosemary noted. She turned to Jeremy. "What just happened – did you really steal the TP? You *actually* pilfered it and took off like a couple of *time fugitives*?"

"Like that's a thing!" laughed Alistair, hands on his hips. "Well, I suppose it *is* now. I like that ... hmm ... Anyway, you're one to talk!"

"What do you mean?"

"You stole it too and came after us. Or *will* come after … us …"

"We what?" Joanne uncrossed her arms and took a deep breath. She sat down at the crying woman's now empty chair and tried to compose herself. "Just start at the beginning, boys. And then you both might think about having a very long shower." She held her nose to make her point.

"All right," said Alistair. Jeremy sat down beside the TP, clutching his satchel as though someone was going to steal it. Rosemary giggled at the irony and looked up at the large set piece; it certainly had a presence about it. She could feel the warmth of its engines from where she was standing as the green lights faded. It was mesmerising. Both girls listened intently to what Alistair had to tell them.

"When we found the TP, we did intend to wait for you before we took pictures and things, but then we found the Golden Knob, and when it fit in the slot it was like all our Valentine's days had come at once, and then when we saw that the inside is exactly how it is on the show and not just an empty shell then, well one of us must have pushed a few buttons or something because the next thing we knew, we woke up at ZealCon, but ZealCon *2005*." He took a deep breath and continued. "It took us a while to figure it out and we had the mother, father and great aunt of all hangovers ... far too much Rampunzel Champunzel and –"

"I have no idea what you're talking about. Can you speak more plainly, please?" Rosemary begged him. "So, one of you messed around with the controls which turned out to be *real working controls*, you both passed out in a drunken stupor and you woke up in 2005?" She turned to Joanne and raised an eyebrow.

"It was a long time ago – relatively speaking – but that's just about the gist of it, yes."

"But we didn't just go back to 2005," Jeremy piped up. He reeled off a list, perfectly from memory: "We went to 1963 to see the Beatles, 1613 to meet William Shakespeare, 1818 to dine with the Prince Regent, 1865 to visit Thomas Crapper, 1604 to have a beer with Guy Fawkes, 1906 to have a coffee with Edwin Hubble ... "

"You met all of those people?" Rosemary gasped, in awe.

"There's more. After that I er ... snuck away to visit Christmas. And that's just the beginning." Alistair disclosed his tatty autograph book and waved it in the air, triumphantly.

"Hang on, hang on …" Joanne interrupted him. "So, what you're saying is that you took this beautiful machine back through time to … to add to your autograph collection?"

Rosemary mouthed to herself, *visit Christmas?*

Jeremy and Alistair looked at each other and shrugged. "Well, yeah, what else do you think we would use it for? No one has autograph collections like ours," said Alistair.

"I don't know if that's ingenious or incredibly, incredibly stupid." Rosemary could not help but agree. They had certainly taken on an admirable feat.

"As I said, you two are ones to talk. You're the ones who followed us. But I don't know how you knew where we were going because … oh …" He turned to his friend. "Nice one, Mr. Encyclopaedia *big mouth* Britannica!"

"I'm sorry," said Jeremy, quietly. "Anyway, you know it all worked out for the best anyway," he said with a wink. His face turned suddenly red under the glares of Rosemary and Joanne.

"So even if we *do* believe you," contemplated Joanne, "what are we going to say to the woman who is responsible for the TP?"

"That she would get a lot of money for this thing on eBay?" Alistair suggested with a mischievous grin. "It definitely passed its road test. And it's quite fast."

"I wonder if she knew that it actually works," Rosemary said.

"I wonder if anyone else knows," pondered Joanne.

"So many questions," Alistair agreed. "Anyway, it's all yours. We are going for some much-needed sleep."

"What – you're not going to stop them from taking it?" Jeremy asked him.

"What's the point?" asked Alistair. "We know that they do and I'm far too tired to argue about it now. Have fun, girls." He reached into his pocket, approached Joanne and handed her the Golden Knob. "Take it, don't take it. Take it next ZealCon. It's your call …"

Joanne looked down at the Knob and turned it over in her hands, golden light glinting in her eyes. It was heavier than she expected it to be. This was no cheap, plastic counterfeit. She gulped, looked at Rosemary and then up at the two men. Her words were quiet, measured.

"It … it's really real isn't it?"

"Oh yes. Really, really real!" said Alistair with a bow and the two of them sauntered away. It would have been a mysterious saunter if Jeremy had not tripped over his boot laces on the way.

Joanne continued to sit there, unmoving, numb and not sure what to do. Her eyes were fixed on the gleaming, gilded object. Was this the missing jigsaw piece in the puzzle that was her life, or was it false hope? A prank or just another piece of disappointment? Joanne was aware that she appeared to be in control of her life, oozing confidence and turning heads as soon as she walked into a room. In comparison with a lot of her contemporaries, she always knew what to say and when to say it and laughed off her own blunders without dwelling on them. But deep down, very deep down, if she stopped to think about it too long, she knew that she wasn't as in control as she made out.

Joanne didn't know where she was going with her life. She was in her twenties and running around corridors barefoot and wearing wings that she had spent weeks making for herself and eating nachos for dinner. Most of her friends back home had children of their own who were doing those kinds of things. Her friends all seemed to know what they were doing, whether it was being full-time parents or climbing the career ladder in their chosen vocation. Joanne didn't really have a chosen vocation. She enjoyed sewing and creating things, but putting limits on the creative arts in a full-time role in a building somewhere just seemed like a contradiction to her. She had her fashion degree under her belt, but even the course had seemed like too much of a restraint on her creativity. Her parents had told her not to worry and that the right job would "come along" soon enough. But in the meantime, she felt as though she was running out of time, missing out on opportunities. Her youth was slipping away from her and she felt powerless to stop it.

Could this be an opportunity for her? An opportunity for adventure and excitement and a few laughs along the way?

"Jo," Rosemary's voice broke into her thoughts. "Are you ready?"

"Am I ... am I ready?" she asked, quietly.

"Yeah. The TP is waiting for us and we should leave before that woman decides to come back."

"But ... you felt *sorry* for that woman, Rosie."

"You're right. Next year?"

"We should do what we came to ZealCon to do – to collect autographs."

"How will we know where we're going?"

Rosemary pointed at Joanne's bulging tote bag. "Asks the one who owns the book of co-ordinates!"

4

"I like the idea of using the time machine to go back through history to collect autographs," mused Joanne. "But first, there's somewhere else I'd like to go."

"Where's that?" asked Rosemary as she closed the door behind her in the small, metallic space.

Joanne said nothing, leafed through the book of co-ordinates, wrinkled up her nose and pondered for a few moments. She clicked her fingers, pressed a few buttons, pulled a few levers and the machine whirred into life all around them. Rosemary held onto the sides in order to keep from falling over. A few excited moments passed inside the TP.

"I hope that this works, with the slight adjustments that I made to the co-ordinates."

"You watch that programme far too closely. I never notice such details. Anyway, I ask again; *where are we?*" Rosemary demanded. Joanne swung open the door.

"The Victoria Suite."

"You moved the TP two rooms to the south?" huffed Rosemary.

"Two rooms to the south *and one year into the future* – less a day or so," Joanne proclaimed. "In other words, ZealCon 2013 should be in full swing in the Elizabeth Suite. If we sneak out into the back corridor through that door over there, in through another door and through where the Faerie Gathering is held, we should be able to get into the con and stave off the old post-con blues for a bit longer. We're already in costume after all."

"It could be fun, I suppose," said Rosemary with a smile. "The weekend went far too quickly. Let's do it." They stepped out, hearts pounding with a mixture of excitement and apprehension.

"It's strange not knowing anything about the guest list for this year," Joanne remarked. "We don't have an itinerary in place at all!"

The girls were pleased to find that the door at the back of the room was unlocked and they slipped through. They looked along a long, unremarkable service corridor and began to make their way down it when they were suddenly apprehended.

"Excuse me, ladies." A man addressed them. He was dressed in the uniform of a hotel employee. He had dark eyes, a goatee and a muscular frame rippled beneath a crisp, white shirt. His name badge informed them that his name was Amir. He crossed his arms and eyed the pair.

"This area of the hotel is reserved for hotel staff only," he told them.

"Oh, I'm sorry Amir," said Joanne. She pulled at a lock of her hair and played with it in a bid to appear innocent. "We got a bit lost and thought this might be the way to the Faerie Gathering."

"Please go back the way you came and refer to the map on the wall in the main corridor. Or your convention programme. I assume that you have one?"

The girls looked at each other.

"We left them in our room," said Rosemary. It was then that she noticed another badge pinned to Amir's waistcoat. "Is that … is that a *Sir Cuthbert's Remarkable Adventures Through Time* badge?" she asked him. "We love that programme."

"Yes, yes it is. I'm quite a fan of the show myself." Amir appeared to relax a little, as though he had forgotten why he had stopped the trespassers. "I thought it would be rather fitting to wear it, considering that it's ZealCon weekend."

"It's *very* cool," said Joanne who was brave enough to reach out and examine the badge for herself. Amir flinched a little at her touch "I don't recognise the design though. It looks different … is that a number *12*?"

"Well, yes, it's the logo for Series 12 of course. I thought you said you were fans?"

"We are, we've just sort of … lost touch lately," Joanne faltered.

Amir coughed. "Anyway, I would appreciate it if you were to go back through the Victoria Suite and enter the convention through the proper entrance."

"OK." Rosemary sighed and they retreated back into the room where the TP stood. "Shall we go back another ten minutes in time to before Amir is doing his rounds?"

"He'll probably still be lurking around. Anyway, I'm not sure that I can be that accurate with the timing – I would need more practice!" Joanne admitted.

"Well, what shall we do then?"

"Why don't we go back out and into the bar and see who is about? We don't need a ticket for that."

"All right," Rosemary shrugged. "But I can barely afford 2012 bar prices let alone 2013 prices."

"Don't worry. My birthday just came around again – I'll see if I've left anything in my account and use the lobby cash machine."

"I don't think your future-self will forgive you!"

"She rarely does!" Joanne laughed. She opened the door and just as quickly, closed it again.

"What? What's wrong?"

"I just saw *you.*"

"What? In the bar?"

"Yes. We can't go out there."

"Why aren't I in the Faerie Gathering? Anyway … I'm sure future us will understand. If we come to next year's con, then we'll know that 2012 us were here too and so we wouldn't be surprised."

"Maybe not, but everyone else *would* be."

"Ah, you have a point."

Joanne paused. "I have a better idea. I know what I can spend my birthday money on as well!"

"What?"

"Let's go back to the TP. One more trip in the future and then it's your turn. I promise."

The TP landed in an unfamiliar, empty warehouse. They exited and Joanne locked up using the Golden Knob.

"Beautiful!" Rosemary commented sarcastically, surveying the environment.

"This isn't it," laughed Joanne. "You'll recognise where we are in a minute. Sure enough, when they reached the main road, Rosemary recognised the shops and eateries which she knew to be a few hundred metres away from the Ballington Hotel. "In here." Joanne took her hand and led her into one of the shops. She looked at the walls which were adorned with designs and painted markings.

"A tattoo shop? You used the TP to travel to a *tattoo shop?*"

"Not just any old tattoo shop," said Joanne and pointed to a poster above the counter. "Look – they have a special offer on; buy one get one half price. I was thinking about getting the new Series 12 logo on my neck. It's lush. Are you in?"

"No, I'm not!" Rosemary said, adamantly.

"Oh." Joanne was obviously disappointed.

"I'm not against other people having them or anything, it's just that I can't think of anything that I would want inked onto my skin *forever*. And there's the small fact that it would hurt."

"Not even if it's my treat?" Joanne took out her purse.

Rosemary shook her head. "It's not going to hurt any less, just because someone else has paid for it. I don't mind waiting while you get it done. But if it's agony – don't blame me."

"Fine." Joanne spoke to the man at the desk and explained what she wanted. He nodded, took out his phone, tapped away on it and scrolled down. "Yes, that one!" Joanne stopped him. She clapped excitedly.

The man went to print off a picture of the logo while Joanne waited.

Sometime later, they emerged from the shop. There was a bandage over the back of Joanne's neck.

"You look like you've been bitten by a vampire," Rosemary told her. "Does it hurt?"

"I'm glad that it's over, put it that way." Joanne winced.

"Wait here and I'll get us a drink and a cake to take your mind off it," Rosemary said and ducked inside a coffee shop.

"Where to, then?" Joanne asked, taking the book of co-ordinates out of her bag."

"I'm still trying to process this. I still don't quite believe that this will work. Do you?"

Joanne nodded, although Rosemary wasn't sure if she was trying to convince her or herself.

"Ok. Well ... Where was it that the boys said they went?" asked Rosemary.

"1963, 1613, 1818 ..."

"Ah yes, 1613. I would *love* to meet William Shakespeare. What do you think, Joanne?"

"Well, it's your turn to choose somewhere. Why not? I've always loved Stratford. Especially in the summertime. Although it does get very busy with all the tourists. Still, I don't suppose you can complain about tourists when you *are* one," she snorted.

"I suppose that would make us *time tourists*," Joanne mused as she programmed the TP.

"Time tourists, ultimate autograph hunters, faeries – the perfect life choices!"

The TP hummed into life and Rosemary wondered what delights were in store for them in Tudor England. Her stomach flipped at the prospect of treading in the footsteps of Shakespeare and his ilk. When Joanne opened the TP door, the flip quickly escalated into a lurch as she clamped her hand to her mouth. What was that *smell*? The answer presented itself when her bare foot stepped down into a river of cold, thick sewage.

Joanne locked the door with one hand and held her nose with other and when she spoke, her voice came out in nasal tones. "Why didn't we choose costumes which required wellies?"

"It's going to take ages to wash this muck off," said Rosemary, looking down at her own submerged feet.

Joanne tentatively removed her hand from her nose and said in a mock Queen's English accent, "I can distinctly detect the aroma of faeces, rotting meat and tanning, with notes of body odour."

"With a lavender finish," added Rosemary in similar tones. She reverted to her usual London accent. "Ugh. I think someone around here must have been trying to mask the stench by over-dosing on perfume. Crikey!"

"Well. One thing's for sure. I've definitely lost my appetite now." The two girls walked down the alleyway where they had landed the TP and across a damp, cobbled street and down an incline which instinctively led to the river.

"I think I can see the river Avon," said Rosemary, pointing. "We can't be far from where Shakespeare lived. I vaguely remember my aunt pointing his house out to me when we went on a theatre trip one Christmas. The whole town was decorated with festive lights – it was quite magical. It looked quite different to this though."

"Is there a tourist information booth anywhere? Perhaps we can get a guidebook," Joanne laughed.

"Tudor England isn't as pretty as I expected it to be," said Rosemary in dismay. "It's quite bleak."

"Oh, I don't know!" Joanne nudged her as a troupe of brightly dressed people rounded the corner of an apothecary, their feet moving in a kind of dance, made all the more bizarre by the splashing of sewage beneath their feet. One of them was carrying a lute, which he presently began to play and the whole group started to sing as they went. One of them winked at the girls and Rosemary found that she was blushing. "They look pretty jolly. Shall we follow them?" asked Joanne.

"They'll probably expect us to tip them," said Rosemary. "I've seen enough street performers to know that they don't do it for their own amusement.

"Why don't we hire a rowing boat and enjoy the river then? Did they have the boat hire back in Tudor times?"

"Even if they did, I think I would rather be inside in the warm. Let's do what we came here to do and collect the autograph, shall we?"

"You're right," Joanne conceded. "We can hire a boat any time in our own time."

The girls located and approached what they hoped was the correct house. They laughed about how absurd the situation was and wondered whether they'd be laughed at, shooed away or even arrested for daring to ask for such a favour from someone so well respected. Wiping their feet desperately on a patch of grass, they knocked and waited. When the door opened, the girls knew instantly that they had found the right house.

Trying to keep her composure, Joanne opened her mouth to speak. But it was the playwright who spoke first. "I've made my donation this month, thank you very much. Run along, now."

"Donation?" asked Joanne.

"Alas, I am not in the giving vein today."

Recognising the *Richard III* quote, Rosemary returned with, "The purest treasure mortal times afford is spotless reputation – that away, men are but gilded loam, or painted clay." Joanne simply looked at her. Rosemary went on, "however, we have not come for coin. Only to beseech of you, your moniker, sir." She held out her autograph book. Rosemary's face was so devoid of expression that Joanne did not know how serious she was being. Was she mocking the great playwright or just playing along? William did not seem to be offended, however, and a broad grin spread across his face as he ushered the girls inside.

"Come on in out of the cold and I will make tea and sign your books."

"Thank you, sir!" said Joanne, gratefully.

"I wish I'd brought along my copy of the *Complete Works of Shakespeare* to get signed," Rosemary whispered.

"*Complete?*" hissed Joanne. "I think it would contain a few spoilers!"

No sooner had they been invited into the drawing room when there came another knock at the door. Shakespeare frowned.

"Are there more of you? I don't normally get this many visitors." He gestured to two chairs and went back out of the room.

The girls laughed. Of course they didn't know anyone else here. Unless … A recognisable voice rang down the hallway.

"This is my brother … Jezab … I mean, Jeremy."

The girls looked at each other and mouthed, "Alistair?" They remained silent and listened.

"I was just telling Mr Shakespeare that I was looking for my – our – young sisters who seemed to have wandered off. We're part of the same … acting troupe … and it's not fair for them to trouble Mr Shakespeare in his resting years."

"I'm not gone yet!" came William's voice. "It is a pleasant treat to see such enthusiasm in the youth. Your costumes are magnificent. I'm intrigued as to what kind of a story should involve two faeries, a well-dressed gentleman and a … er … what are you dressed as, boy?"

"A boot polisher, Mr Shakespeare, sir."

"Quite!"

The girls heard the front door close and the voices got nearer.

"Here we are," the playwright announced on his return. Indeed, it was Alistair with his friend Jeremy in tow. William left the room again and promised to return with tea.

"He doesn't speak how I expected him to either," Alistair whispered as he and Jeremy sat down.

"Well how did you expect him to speak? You wouldn't expect Dr Seuss to speak in rhyme all the time, do you?"

"Yeah ... yeah I would actually."

"What are you two doing here?" Joanne finally asked. Although she knew perfectly well that this was no coincidence. She nudged Rosemary and hoped that she would play along.

"What are *we* doing here?" hissed Alistair. "What are *you two* doing here – nonchalantly parading around 16th-century England and dropping in on William Shakespeare for tea and scones?"

"The same thing as us, I expect," said Jeremy, flatly. He pointed at Rosemary who was clutching an autograph book and pen.

"I don't believe this – you not only followed us, but you copied us! This was *our* idea!" grumbled Alistair.

"*We* followed *you*?" asked Rosemary, "I think you'll find that we were here first."

Joanne stifled a laugh. The look on Alistair's face was priceless.

"But how did you get here?" asked Alistair.

"If you're going to do this properly, then don't forget to hold back on the anachronisms wherever possible," said Jeremy, who took a quill from a sturdy-looking writing desk. "I don't think the ball-point pen was invented yet!"

"That's nothing," Joanne laughed raucously and said in whispered tones, "She wanted to get him to sign *The Complete Works of Shakespeare*!"

Their host appeared with a tea tray which he set down on the coffee table.

"I see that you've forgiven your younger sisters then, if the sound of mirth is anything to go by."

"We've what?" asked Alistair. Remembering his story, he followed quickly with, "Ah yes, but they shall not go unpunished."

Joanne gasped at his cheek as William went about the business of serving drinks to the unexpected guests. The party made light conversation about the playwright's work, acting and the theatre.

Rosemary could not help but feel awkward, dressed as she was, so far from home and in such unusual circumstances. The surreality of the situation had suddenly hit her as she sipped her hot tea. What were they doing, messing around travelling to such a significant place and time? One wrong word and history could be changed forever. Couldn't it? What if they did something wrong and they couldn't get back and they were stuck in Tudor times forever? What if they caught a disease that hadn't yet got a cure or they got thrown in gaol for stealing bread because they had become so lost and hungry? What if they became separated and she got stuck somewhere on her own?

Rosemary shook her head, willing the anxiety monster to leave her alone. This was an *adventure*. She was only drinking tea with her best friend and they could leave any time they wanted to. Having become lost in her thoughts, Rosemary realised that her cup was empty and that there was a flourish of paper as the others asked William for his signature. Rosemary waited her turn and held out her book with a shaking hand, as the great writer wrote his autograph in meticulous script. She thanked him and Joanne went so far as to shake the man's hand.

As they finished their tea and bade their farewells, Alistair hissed, "I don't recall you having that tattoo last time I saw you."

"Er … we should be getting along, Rosemary," Joanne said awkwardly. She grabbed hold of Rosemary's hand and they began to flee. Alistair and Jeremy ran after them.

Alistair called after them, but instead of turning back they continued to run through the filthy Tudor streets.

"Well, that was all a bit crazy," puffed Rosemary as they neared the TP.

"It was a scream!" Joanne squealed. "Did you see the looks on their faces? I wish I could have taken a photograph. They were so annoyed that we had got there first – even though it was them that told us they came here."

"And we only went there because they told us that. Agh." Rosemary tapped her head with her hand. "Paradoxes really mess with my head. It's why I prefer fantasy over sci-fi."

"You'll get used to it," Joanne said casually.

"I very much doubt it."

It was Joanne's turn to choose where their adventures took them next. She checked her tattoo bandage by feel and winced. It wasn't ready to be removed just yet. Her friend had been rather quiet since they had left Stratford and she didn't want to upset her by bumping purposefully into Jeremy and Alistair again yet either. *What would cheer her up?* she wondered. Rosemary liked comedy, didn't she? Particularly vintage comedy which she used to enjoy watching with her dad as a child, one silent film franchise in particular. Joanne knew exactly where to go. Consulting the book of co-ordinates, she programmed the TP to go to where Sir Cuthbert had once travelled. And to where their clothes were more suited.

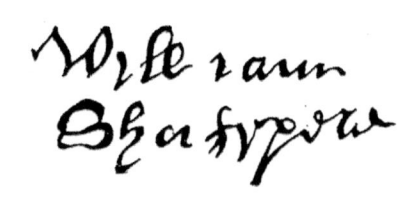

6

"This looks like ... it looks like a Hollywood film set," said Rosemary as she stepped out onto a sandy pavement.

"Santa Monica Beach!"

"Of course!" Rosemary exclaimed. "Look – there's the pier that you see in all those films ... although it hasn't got the iconic big wheel. Why hasn't it got it the iconic big wheel?" she whined.

Joanne laughed at her diction. "Because the *iconic big wheel* hasn't been built yet of course. Its 1957.

"1957? Hmm ... I think I'm going to need another clue."

"OK. You're probably used to seeing this person with their other half of a pair."

"A famous Hollywood couple?"

"I said *pair*. You would also not be used to seeing him in full colour."

"I know! *I know!* Its Stan Laurel, isn't it? He moved here after Oliver Hardy died at about this time." Rosemary threw her arms around Joanne. "What a great idea! It's so bright and sunny and warm. I don't know how anyone could ever be sad here."

"I don't know about that, Rosemary. You have to be quite well off to live here. I heard that someone in a minimum wage job needs three full-time jobs just to survive," said Joanne in dismay. "Los Angeles is a strange place. I'm not sure how I feel about it to be honest." Then she remembered that she was supposed to be cheering her friend up, not depressing her. So she added, "Well at least we didn't have to pay the air fare to visit. *Or* fork out to stay in an expensive hotel."

This is so exciting, Jo! Hang on though," Rosemary paused. "If its 1957, do you think Stan will be grieving? It can't be much of a happy place for *him* at this time."

"I don't know. But I saw on a documentary once that though he retired at sixty-five, Stan wasn't a recluse. He actually *welcomed* people round to his home and told them anecdotes and kept them entertained for hours. Rosemary, we could be two of those people!"

"I saw that documentary too! And my dad bought me a book about Laurel and Hardy two Christmases ago. The books says that Stan's address was in a regular phonebook. He was one of the most famous people on the planet at the time, with over a hundred films under his belt, and he wasn't even ex-directory! Now, what was his address? Damn, I re-read that book in February. Why can't I remember?"

"Well let's find a phone box and find out. There's bound to be one around here somewhere."

Joanne locked the door of the TP with the Golden Knob and brushed a few branches in front of the door in a bid to hide it among the foliage of the tree they had landed next to. The machine was still quite conspicuous, with hints of brass and silver glinting through the leaves, but this was Hollywood, where anything was possible. Or that was what Joanne tried to convince herself, at least. They headed along the long, wide street known as Ocean Avenue, which ran parallel with the seafront. The road was lined with palm trees at equidistant intervals and banked with stores, apartments and eateries. It was busy, but not as bustling as Joanne might have imagined. There were no Segway-riding or cycling tourists on their way to the beach and no roller-blading or jogging locals sporting little more than a bikini and a tan. Rather, the populace was more modestly dressed and there was a certain air of sophistication.

"I suppose our costumes must look out of place after all," Joanne noted.

"Fast forward to the sixties and we might get away with it," said Rosemary, who was having a job keeping up with her friend. She added, "that looks like it might be one of those phone booths," and pointed to a glass and metallic construction on an intersection. She rushed ahead of Joanne and swung open the door. A well-thumbed directory was resting on a shelf next to an old-fashioned telephone and Rosemary started immediately to leaf through it.

"Laurel, Laurel, Laurel," she muttered as she flicked through the pages. She scanned the listings and ran her finger down one of the thin pages. "Stanley Laurel, Venice Beach … Stanley Laurel, Hermosa Beach … Ah, here we are! This must be it. 1111 Franklin Street, Santa Monica.

"Well done!" Joanne beamed and gave her a high five.

"Now, which way?"

Rosemary was barely out of the booth when Joanne stopped a passer-by, a glamourous middle-aged woman wearing a fur coat and sunglasses, and asked her for directions.

"Why, it's about thirty blocks that way," the woman informed her, and pointed up a street which led away from the coast. Her fingernails were long and red.

"How far *is* that?" Joanne asked.

"You'll probably need to take a cab," said the woman. "It's about two, maybe three miles."

"Oh, I'm sure we can manage that on foot."

The woman tilted her sunglasses and looked over the frames at the barefoot girls before her. "You're not from around here, are you, sweetie?"

"Not exactly. Thanks for the directions." Joanne gave a little wave, grabbed Rosemary's arm and steered her away. "Come on. We've got our own transport."

"I never thought of that. I was just thinking about all those miles on my poor feet. Why didn't we pack shoes, Jo?"

"They wouldn't go with our outfits. Anyway, let's just get going, shall we?"

Rosemary shrugged and they walked all the way back to the TP. Once inside, Joanne punched in the new co-ordinates and moments later they were on Franklin Street. Only it couldn't have been moments later because when Rosemary swung open the door it was dark.

"Oh great. Is it night-time already? And *which* night? Is it still even 1957?"

"I don't think it's night. Our voices sound strange – as though we're indoors."

They felt around for a wall, furniture, anything that could give them a clue of their whereabouts.

"I hope we haven't landed in his bedroom," Rosemary whispered. "I mean, I like the guy, but not like *that*."

"Aha!" exclaimed Joanne. "I think I can feel something car-shaped."

"And I can feel something light-switch-shaped." Rosemary flicked on the light and she saw that Joanne indeed had her hand on a shiny red automobile with immaculate bodywork and impressive fins.

"I would move away from that if I were you," Rosemary warned. "That looks like a '57 Chevy. I doubt the owner would want fingerprints all over it!"

Joanne whistled with admiration as she took it in. It was quite a specimen for such a small, humble garage. She located the way out and they found themselves in a cluttered, narrow hallway. The furnishings and fixtures gave off a light scent which hit Joanne's olfactory system in the way that her gran's house did, but she couldn't put her finger on what that scent was exactly.

"Hang on," whispered Rosemary. "We can't just waltz into his living room, unannounced. We don't even know if we've got the right house."

"I was planning on doing the lambada actually," Joanne quipped. "No, you're right. Let's sneak outside and knock on the door."

The girls crept back into the garage and hauled up the large swing-door and let themselves out the front before locating the front door proper. Joanne rang the bell. There was a long pause and the girls were about to give up waiting when the door finally opened.

"Why hello there, can I help you young ladies?" The door was answered by a man of around five feet six. He did not appear elderly, but his skin hinted at a life well lived; his eyes implied that they had seen many interesting sights and the furrows on his brow suggested that he had many stories to tell.

"Hello there, Mr ... Mr Laurel," Rosemary stammered, suddenly nervous. "We are big fans of yours and were just passing."

Joanne stifled a laugh at the idea of that.

"And ..." Rosemary continued.

"Say, I've just fixed some fresh lemonade and I've made far too much. Would you girls like to try some?"

"Yes please," said Rosemary.

"Swell. Just come on in and I'll go fetch it. It's a mighty warm day again so we may as well sit out back."

The girls hustled through the door and looked around, pretending it was the first time they had been inside his home.

"Say, you girls didn't happen across a raccoon or a cat or anything did you?"

"No, why?" asked Joanne.

"I thought I heard something just a moment ago out front. Might've got into the garage or something like that. Never mind. Here's the lemonade." The girls thanked him for the cool, brimming glasses which he handed them and followed him through the house and onto a patio area. "Do take a seat. So, what are your names?"

"Rosemary."

"Joanne."

"Stanley Laurel, at your service. Say, do I detect British accents?"

"Yes, we're from England," said Rosemary.

"Wonderful place," he said and sipped his drink.

Rosemary could not help but stare at the iconic film actor. He didn't look quite right without his bowler hat and partner at his side. He took a cigarette packet from his pocket and offered it to his guests. Both girls declined but he proceeded to light one for himself without question. The next two hours were like a dream to Rosemary, for their host went on to talk at length about his adventures with Oliver Hardy – both on- and offscreen, and completely unprompted by the girls. They simply listened, wide eyed and open mouthed. At one point he paused, took a handkerchief from his top pocket and dabbed at his eyes.

"Do excuse me, ladies. It's only been a couple of months after all."

Rosemary and Joanne looked at each other with expressions of genuine pity on their faces.

"Of course," said Rosemary. "If it's too painful for you to talk about him then please don't upset yourself, Mr Laurel. We only came along to meet you and didn't expect all of this hospitality."

"That's mighty sweet of you, Miss. But not talking about him won't make the hurt go away, so I'll continue if I may. Did I tell you yet about how Oliver showed up to my wedding late? I've been married precisely four times you know." Stanley sniffed and lit his fourth cigarette that afternoon.

The afternoon drew on and Joanne visibly shivered under her thin fairy costume.

"The evening is drawing in. Shall we go on inside?" Stan asked, standing up. "I can fix us some fresh lemonade."

"That's very kind, but we've taken up too much of your time already," said Rosemary. "But before we go – please can you sign our autograph books for us?"

"Why, certainly," he said with a smile and signed each book as they were placed on the patio table.

"We can let ourselves out," Joanne said quickly as she stowed her book in her bag.

"You girls take care now." He made his way back through the house and into the kitchen while the girls slipped through the side door and into the garage before Stan could question their whereabouts.

"This autograph-hunting lark is easy," said Joanne as the TP thrummed out of 1957 America.

"Yeah, that was sick!" Rosemary enthused, staring at the latest addition to her autograph collection. "Where are we going next? It's your turn, isn't it?"

"Well, that one was technically my turn, but I chose Stan for you."

"I know." Rosemary shrugged. "But I think you should choose one for you anyway."

"I already have done," said Joanne with a grin.

"Where are we going?"

"Back to Britain. To meet up with the boys."

"Not at ZealCon already? I mean again … er …"

"No, no. In Brighton Pavilion where they met the Prince Regent. I can't wait to see the looks on their faces when they see us!" Joanne's laughter echoed inside the TP.

"But they already know we went there."

"Oh, the Jeremy and Alistair in the *present* know. But back in 1613 they were surprised to see us, weren't they? And therefore they will be surprised in 1818 too. It's the gift that keeps on giving. It'll be hilarious!"

"I see what you mean. I think. Right. Let's go!"

"Brighton Bound!"

Stan Laurel.

7

"Are we really at Brighton Pavilion?" Rosemary enthused.

Joanne nodded with confidence. "I just hope we've landed somewhere inconspicuous and not in the middle of a ballroom or something. Hmm … it seems quiet enough out there. Open the door. You're nearest."

"Yes, by about two inches. It's hardly a mansion in here!" Rosemary creaked open the door just wide enough for a peek, thoroughly prepared to slam it shut again.

"It doesn't look very palatial out there either. Could be another cupboard." She dared to open the door wider. The scent of musty upholstery hit them as they disembarked. "Servants quarters perhaps? Judging by all the cobwebs and the state of the windows, I don't think this room's been used for a while." Rosemary couldn't even see out of the small windows which were so thick with grime that barely any daylight could get through. Joanne locked up the TP, walked over to a solitary single bed and thumped it. A layer of dust jumped up, as thick as a bedsheet. She coughed.

"I think you're right. No one is going to come in here."

"I think we should probably leave these things behind for this one," said Rosemary, taking off her wings.

Joanne agreed and followed suit.

Rosemary tugged at the door of a wooden wardrobe which was so warped that the piece would give the Leaning Tower of Pisa a run for its money. The wardrobe jolted open, but not without nearly toppling onto her. She scrambled around for a bedsheet which she proceeded to throw over the TP in a vague attempt to hide it.

"Might help a bit," she said with a shrug as she stared at the barely concealed strange shape in the corner of the room. Joanne simply pocketed the Golden Knob and strode out of the room and down the corridor as though she were in her own home. When she opened the door at the end of the corridor, however, she stopped in her tracks. She turned to Rosemary and said in a whisper, "Wow. I don't think I've seen luxury like it! I mean, I've visited stately homes before where everything is luxurious and expensive-looking, but it's often faded and worn. Actually being somewhere like this in its heyday is something else!"

"I see what you mean!" Rosemary gasped as she followed her out onto a large, ornate landing. Shutting the door behind her, Rosemary found that it closed flush with the wall and was adorned with the same textured wallpaper as the rest of the wall, making it almost hidden from sight. "Clever!"

The landing was empty and the girls took in the scene. The ceiling was made of glass and trimmed with iron and gold. The burgundy coving was a prominent feature which added to the grandiosity of the high walls. Finely detailed figures were painted onto windowpanes opposite them and golden bannisters led down the wide staircase and into an equally opulent hallway. Every detail was deliberate and beautiful. Each piece of furniture and every nook had been painstakingly crafted to perfection, leaving no space untouched by luxury. It was as though King Midas had run through the palace, touching everything in his path. Joanne absent-mindedly placed a hand on the banister and began walking down the stairs, as though on a mission.

"Where are we going?" hissed Rosemary, suddenly panicking. "Surely there are guards around. What if they're armed? *What are we doing, Jo?*"

"Relax," said Joanne. "Follow my lead."

"How do you know where Alistair and Jeremy are going to be? By the looks of it, this place is huge!" Rosemary hissed.

Just then, a figure appeared at the bottom of the staircase. But he was no armed guard and he was markedly older and better dressed than either Alistair or Jeremy. He was, in fact, a regal-looking gentleman and it looked as though his dressing room had thrown up on him. He was draped in the most fantastic finery that the girls had ever seen, weighed down with colourful sashes and chains and ornamental pieces, topped by a flowing velvet cape. He was not a small man underneath all of his garments and his very presence filled the entire hallway, indeed the entire palace. A wonky collar and ruffled hair, although quite jarring in the overall effect, only added an air of eccentricity to the vision of him.

"Are you looking for the ladies' parlour?" he greeted them. The girls looked at each other and both gave an awkward mid-staircase curtsey. Before they had a chance to respond he said, "I must say, the outfits that the young folk wear in London really are becoming more and more remarkable."

"Delighted to meet you, Your Highness," Rosemary said, hoping against all hope that she was not mistaken; could this be the Prince Regent? The gentleman squinted at Rosemary, looking her up and down in a way which made her feel uncomfortable. "And how *exotic* you are, Lady … Lady …"

"Rosemary, Your Highness." She padded down the last few steps and curtseyed again. Rosemary bit her tongue on hearing his choice of words, which she expected had been used due to the colour of her skin. She had heard much worse and suspected that he meant no malice, especially considering it was 1818, but it still grated on her all the same, prince or no prince. To her surprise, the prince took the liberty of taking her hand and kissing it, leaving a trace scent of liquor behind. She noticed Joanne visibly cringing beside her as she also offered another curtesy.

"Joanne, Your Highness," Joanne said and received the same boozy greeting. It was then that they realised how unsteady he was on his feet. It wasn't the sheer weight of his garments that were making him sway. He was quite obviously utterly and completely drunk.

"Magnificent. Delighted to meet you. And I trust that you become acquainted with your rooms? I expect that my staff have been looking after you since your arrival?"

"Well," started Rosemary. Joanne kicked her lightly on the ankle and interjected, "Of course. We have been looking forward to visiting for quite some time."

"You'll forgive me for not knowing your names just now." The prince took the liberty of putting an arm around each of their shoulders. "So many faces, so many parties, so many feasts …" he waved an arm dismissively. "Sometimes it's as though they all roll into one."

"Of course," said Rosemary again. She felt a little uncomfortable with his arm around her, but was reassured by the fact that Joanne was there too. Was this how people really behaved back then? Or just princes? Or just this *particular* prince?

He steered the girls through several grand archways until they reached a room which the prince described as the Long Gallery. With a swish and a stagger, he left their sides and went off to converse with some of the gentlemen in the room. The girls looked around them in awe. The walls of the long, pink room were adorned with designs of trees, flora and birds and were dramatically lit by a central stained-glass ceiling. As sunset was nearing, the many painted lanterns were also coming into fruition, their light effecting a cosy, yet luxurious, ambiance. The Gallery, with obvious Eastern influences, was festooned with Chinese pieces and furnishings and decor which evoked a bamboo grove. The people who filled the room were beautifully adorned, with not a hair out of place, making Joanne and Rosemary feel like they had crash-landed from another planet, let alone another time.

Three such women who looked as though they had stepped out of one of the paintings which had adorned the grand hallway, approached the lost-looking wingless faeries. Rosemary and Joanne curtseyed awkwardly once more.

"Good evening. I am Lady Jocelyn. This is Lady Mary and Lady Emily."

"Lady Joanne and Lady Rosemary," said Joanne, trying not to laugh at the prospect.

"Of course the prince is far too busy to introduce us himself."

"Or too drunk!" exclaimed Lady Emily with a laugh.

"Too intoxicated to even delegate the simple task to one of his many staff also, it seems," scoffed Lady Mary.

"Oh I don't mind. I'm not too bothered about formalities," said Rosemary.

"Well, we don't all hold the same standards, I suppose," said Lady Mary who was the second person to scrutinise her appearance that day. Rosemary bit her tongue again.

At that moment a member of staff approached them, who Rosemary suspected was a footman. He offered a shining silver plate upon which there were several glasses. The girls each took one, without hesitation, as did the three ladies.

"I do like a free bar!" Joanne whispered and elbowed Rosemary so hard that she spilt some of her drink. "So how do you three know His Highness?" Joanne asked, as though she had just popped by at a neighbour's house party.

Lady Jocelyn raised an eyebrow and said, "We have been acquainted with His Highness for a long while. We were invited for the occasion to meet Sir Francis. Although I'm sure the original invitation was for tomorrow. Thankfully we reside in the county."

"Hah!" Lady Emily scoffed, "we were probably just invited to make up the numbers!"

"Sir Francis?" asked Rosemary.

"Yes, the minister of course. He's down from London for the banquet; the prince's special guest."

"Indeed," said Joanne as she helped herself to another glass from another passing footman.

Yet another footman appeared at the doorway and announced that dinner was served.

The banqueting room was a beautifully decorated space with high windows draped in rich, vibrant curtains. It boasted a high ceiling decorated with gold. chandeliers hung all around, the largest of which was hung directly above the longest dining table that the girls had ever seen. Being a fan of the fantasy genre, Rosemary could not help but be impressed by the heavy dragon imagery in the room's detail.

The gold motif continued onto the large table with glittering goblets, platters and candlesticks. Rosemary counted twenty-five dining chairs set around the table, with a throne-like seat positioned half-way down the length.

One of the footmen greeted Rosemary and led her to a seat to the left of the throne and another led Joanne to a seat to the right of it. It didn't take long for all of the guests to be seated, particularly as each of them appeared to have their own dedicated footman. Joanne was not used to this kind of situation, and would have found it particularly uncomfortable had she not downed two glasses of champagne in the last fifteen minutes. To her delight, the Prince Regent took his seat between them. The prince greeted them both with a warm wink which somehow put Joanne at ease. She thanked her footman as he poured a little red wine into the goblet that was nearest to her. As she took a sip, Joanne spied a familiar face over the brim of the goblet. It was Jeremy.

Rosemary nearly spilled her wine when the prince draped his arm around her and Joanne simultaneously, jolting her. From her position it was impossible to see Joanne's face past the prince's bulk, but she saw the look of surprise on Jeremy's. The prince spoke.

"Sir Frank, may I introduce you to Lady Joanne and Lady Rosemary?"

"Pleased to meet you," said Jeremy, who looked like a stoat caught in the headlights.

"*Sir Frank?*" Joanne asked, trying not to laugh. "You look so ... familiar."

"It comes with the territory, I expect," said the prince. "Sir Frank is an important parliamentarian after all!"

"Of *course!*" said Joanne.

Joanne found herself entertained by Jeremy's confusion. It felt justified after the boys had taken off in the TP without them that day. Where *was* Alistair anyway? She was dying to ask, but didn't want to get the boys into trouble. If Jeremy had somehow been mistaken for an MP, who knew where Alistair was. Perhaps he had ended up in one of the many pies that were being dished out. She laughed at the idea and then admonished herself. This was not television. This was not *Sir Cuthbert's Remarkable Adventures*. This was real. And no amount of wine should be able to convince her otherwise. Anything could go wrong. They had to play it safe. And hopefully that meant remaining on the right side of this unpredictable prince.

Each of the many courses brought with it yet more champagne and Rosemary struggled to keep up. Although it was a leisurely dinner over several hours, it was not easy to make small talk without feeling conspicuous. She found it easier to nod and smile at whatever the prince said and laughed along with the guests, even if she didn't understand the context. She found interest in watching Jeremy and felt sorry for him in a way. What sequence of events had led to him being confused for Sir Francis and where was Alistair? Was he safe?

The prince eventually looked around the room and, apparently satisfied that everyone was satiated, announced that his guests were invited to leave the table.

Both men and women were invited into a saloon which was less fancy than the banqueting room, but just as beautiful in its own way. The well-appointed state room leant itself well to relaxation and after-dinner conversation with its plush furnishings and ample floor space.

Rosemary spotted a musician sitting at a grand piano whose wonderful music only added to the atmosphere. She looked around her to see where the prince was, but recognised only Jeremy, who bounded over to them absurdly in his Sir Cuthbert costume.

"Hello *Sir Frank*," she said with a giggle.

"Hello *Lady Rosemary* and *Lady Joanne*," said Jeremy, but there was no mirth in his tone. "Come on then, tell me what's going on."

"Shall we ask the pianist if he does requests?" giggled Rosemary, knowingly winding up Jeremy.

"I'm the only one who's allowed to evade questions around here," harrumphed Jeremy.

"Oh, come on now, you're not a real politician," said Joanne.

"And you're not really ladies. Well, you are *ladies*, but … well you know what I mean. Please tell me what's going on!" Jeremy looked as though he was going to explode with frustration.

Rosemary looked at Joanne, and then turned back to Jeremy. She rested a hand delicately on his shoulder and smiled sweetly. She leaned in and informed him, "We're hunting for autographs. Like you."

"We established that fact when we went to visit old Willy. But how did you get there? How did you get *here*? We waited for you two to join us at the convention but you didn't turn up. We thought you'd changed your minds or something."

"No, we didn't change our minds. We were busy getting ready. And by the time we eventually found where the TP was, it ... *wasn't*. It had gone!"

"Ah. It wasn't intentional, you know. We didn't know the TP worked ... it was purely serendipitous! Did anyone notice that it had disappeared?" asked Jeremy with a gasp.

"Well yes and no ... the time machine appeared back at the convention on Sunday evening. With you two in it. We have already had this conversation."

"No we haven't," Jeremy insisted.

"Well you *will* have it," said Joanne.

"So ... when we arrived back at the convention, *two days late*, we told you both all about our travels?" asked Jeremy. The girls nodded. "Well at least we get back OK." He thought for a moment. "So who do we meet next? What happens? Where do we go?"

Joanne laughed wildly. "I'm sure we'll see you there!"

"Well ... maybe we *won't* tell you where we went. Then you won't know," said Jeremy.

"I'm not sure that it works like that," said Rosemary, hopefully.

"Even if it does, we obviously found out somehow," added Joanne. She looked around her, suddenly aware that others might be listening in.

"So when did you get the tattoo?" Jeremy asked suddenly. Joanne put her hand on her neck, as if to protect it.

"I got it for my birthday," said Joanne. "It's the new logo for Series 12 –"

"*Jo!*" Rosemary admonished her. Joanne clamped a hand over her mouth. But it was too late.

"What did you say?" asked Jeremy. Without asking permission, he brushed Joanne's long hair aside so that he could have a proper look at the markings. "Is this ... is this the actual logo or is this just speculation?" he asked, seriously.

"Why would I get permanent ink tattooed onto my skin of a logo that was just *speculation*?" Joanne stepped back and covered her neck once more. "Of course it's the actual logo."

"Joanne!" Rosemary hissed.

"Oh it's too late now, Rosie," Joanne sighed. "He's seen it."

"When was the logo revealed and when could you possibly have got the tattoo done? Back in 2012, Series 12 has only just been confirmed. So, the logo would not be revealed until at least a few months later, maybe not even until the first episode was aired!"

Jeremy faltered, tripped over his words and became nonsensical, either due to the champagne or utter confusion. Or possibly both.

The Prince Regent appeared suddenly and he took the liberty of draping an arm around each of the girls again.

"You do sheem to attract the ladies, Sir Frank," the prince slurred. His hefty bulk weighed heavily on the girls' shoulders as his weakened knees buckled under his weight. "The pianisht is playing his final piesh – may I suggesht that we all go through to the mushic room?"

The girls agreed, glad to be finally free from Jeremy's questions. The music room was a great hall, at one end of which a modest orchestra was positioned.

"Of course!" Rosemary exclaimed as the sight of the musicians. "Nothing but the best for an after-party at the Pavilion!"

"Where did all of these extra people come from?" Joanne shouted over the music, suddenly feeling like she was in a nightclub.

"Perhaps they've been queuing all night to get in. I wonder if the palace has bouncers."

"I think the proper term is *guards*," said Joanne. She then said, "I could get used to being called Lady Joanne. How about you, Lady Rosemary? Or do you prefer Lady Rosie?"

"Funnily enough, *Lady Joanne*, I've been thinking about names," said Rosemary. "My mum once told me that I was named after our ancestor, Mary Seacole. Rose*mary*. I don't know how true that is, but she did like to talk about Mary Seacole like she was someone we both knew well."

"In what way?"

"Well, say if I fell off my bike, she would say that Mary Seacole would soon have me patched up like a wounded soldier, but that she would have to do for now. Or if my cousins stayed over, she would joke that our home was just like the British Hotel which Mary ran in the Crimean War."

"I've heard of her," said Joanne. "There's a ward named after her at the hospital near me. I remember looking her up. She was a bit of a heroine, wasn't she? It would be cool if she *was* a relation."

"I've never really doubted it, but then I've never really thought about it that much. I just kind of *accepted* it. I don't suppose I realised how famous she was at the time. She just seemed like some woman my mum used to bang on about. Like she would a neighbour or friend."

Just then, a woman draped in layers and layers of sumptuous fabric sashayed past them. Her apparel took up so much space that the wearer barely noticed that she almost knocked Joanne off her feet. Joanne was so distracted by the lavish dress that she didn't seem to mind.

"Just look at some of the clothes. Have you ever *seen* such beautiful material?"

"There are some very special costumes, I mean *dresses*, here aren't there? I would love to talk to some of the women about them, but I expect they've all had them hand made for them especially. I doubt they would have their own sewing machines or anything."

"Especially since they weren't invented until 1846!"

The girls laughed again, exhausted and slightly merry.

"Well, well. You two seem to be enjoying yourselves, rather!" A gentleman with fair hair, accompanied by a man of Indian heritage, said as they approached the girls. "Care to share the joke with us?"

"Oh, I don't think …" began Rosemary.

"Is it something us men wouldn't understand?" he said, rather condescendingly, Joanne thought.

"Something like that," she said. The two of them stifled their laughter as the gentlemen introduced themselves.

"Sir Crispin and Shree-Ramesh at your service." Sir Crispin and Shree-Ramesh bowed low and the girls curtseyed. Joanne spotted Jeremy in the edge of her vision. He was making a bad show of pretending not to be looking their way. He looked awkward and almost green with envy. Joanne felt a hint of guilt, but quickly tossed the emotion aside. She and Rosemary deserved to have a little fun, didn't they?

"We noticed your proximity to the prince at dinner," said Ramesh. "Good friends of his, are you?"

"Oh, not really," said Rosemary, honestly. "But we were honoured to have been asked to sit with him of course."

"And what a delightful meal it was," said Crispin, suppressing a belch behind a clenched fist. "Although I fear I have had more than a little too much wine!"

"You're not the only one," said Rosemary before she could stop herself. Shree-Ramesh eyed up the girls in a way that made them feel more than a little uncomfortable. "You two *do* look exquisite. I don't care much for what some of the other guests are saying about the pair of you; your outfits emphasise your womanly shapes in a way that probably makes them all green with envy."

"Quite," agreed Crispin, his gaze clearly on Rosemary's chest.

As the musicians came to the end of their piece, the prince announced that supper had been served in the saloon and then promptly stumbled out through the door. The music continued and Rosemary shouted over the hubbub, "I don't think I could eat another thing!"

"Me neither," said Crispin who pulled Joanne towards him and obviously had pursuits other than food on his mind.

"Er, I think I might like to grab something!" said Joanne quickly as she pulled away from him. She grasped Rosemary's hand, wide eyed, and said through gritted teeth, "come and help me choose what to eat, Rosemary darling." Rosemary got the hint and the two of them padded across the music room and in the direction of the saloon.

"You're not still hungry, are you?" Rosemary hissed.

"No of course not. I'm stuffed after all those courses! I just wanted an excuse to get away from their lecherous eyes. Besides, we need to focus on our mission and get our autograph before we're too late."

"At first I thought we could have had some fun, but you're right," agreed Rosemary. "We should be careful. It's all very well flirting, but we don't want to end up being our own great-great-great grandmothers or anything. Anyway, those guys were creeps!"

"Exactly!"

"Ah, there you are," came the Prince Regent's familiar tone. "And how are you beautiful ladeesh enjoying yourselvesh at my little soirée this evening?"

"*Or even the next Queen of England!*" Rosemary whispered to Joanne. The prince was so inebriated that he did not seem to notice her comment.

"We are doing splendidly, Your Highness," Joanne said loudly. "Although we have but one request."

"Of coursh. Ask away!"

"Might we please trouble you for your signature in order for us to be able to remember what a truly wonderful time we have had?"

"Well, I have had one or two ales thish evening, but if I can still hold a pen then I shall indeed try my besht!"

"Well that was fun!" giggled Rosemary as the girls stumbled across the landing in the direction of the servants' corridor.

"Wait!" a voice called behind them. It was Shree-Ramesh. "Where are you fine ladies going? The party is not over."

"Er …" Rosemary scrambled around for an answer, as she didn't think it would be appropriate to tell him that they were about to get into a time machine and travel back to the twenty-first century, or wherever their adventure next took them.

"We are going to change into something more appropriate," Joanne said quickly. "After seeing the delightful gowns all the ladies are wearing, we felt under-dressed, somewhat."

"I see," Ramesh raised an eyebrow and stroked his chin in thought. "But your apparel is your appeal. Sir Crispin and I are rather taken by your exotic attire. Back in my country …"

"We really do need to go and get changed," interjected Joanne. "It's not really the right climate for such clothes and we are starting to feel cold as the evening has gone on –"

Ramesh took a step closer and the girls realised that Crispin had come up the opposite staircase and the two men were bookending them, rendering them trapped.

"Oh, I am sure that we can keep you warm, isn't that right, Shree-Ramesh?" said Crispin, his words thick with sinister undertones.

"That's right, Sir Crispin," came his response, slick and low. Rosemary suddenly started, her voice shrill and defiant.

"You're no *sir* and you're no *shree*. You don't deserve *any* title. You're nothing but a couple of perves! I bet neither of you have bathed for a decade and you'll die as sad, miserable virgins!" Rosemary grabbed Joanne's hand and slipped swiftly through the hidden servants' door. The girls stood panting, with their backs to the door, ensuring they would not be followed. They heard Crispin's voice bellow angrily after them, "I'll have you know that I bathed in June. And I have had a girlfriend!"

The girls looked at each other and melted into laughter.

"Kind of pathetic really," said Joanne once they were sure that the "*gentlemen*" had gone. Joanne gave Rosemary a high five. "Nicely done, Rosie. Well done out there!"

"Well, they needed to be told," said Rosemary. "I don't care if they were sirs, princes or gods, whether they're from 2012, 1818 or 300 BC; men are men and, unfortunately, we still have to have our wits about us."

"Sadly, I think you might be right," sighed Joanne. "Come on, let's get back to the TP and sober up.

"Ugh, it's a bit cramped in there," Rosemary complained. "I know that old bed isn't exactly inviting, but it'd be good to stretch out and have a snooze for a few hours."

"You're right. Help me shift this cupboard in front of the door, just in case someone tries to come in here. A decent sleep does sound like a good idea."

9

Once they had slept off their hangovers in relative comfort, Rosemary and Joanne landed the TP at a campsite so that they could make use of the facilities. The sliver of moon offered little light in the dark field, so the TP simply appeared like a fancy tent in the backdrop of canvas. They had found some clean towels from the on-site pool and had enough coins to use the washing machine. They had been careful to land in the dead of night when they were less likely to be spotted. Or so they thought. For when Joanne was drying her hair, a group of late-night revellers entered the shower block. Rosemary and Joanne, barefoot and dressed in clean, but still damp, faerie costumes simply paid them no mind and went about their business. The revellers looked the girls up and down and made their way to the toilet cubicles, talking and laughing among themselves.

Once they were feeling more human again, the girls stepped back into the TP. Out of all the places they could have gone to for a nice warm shower or a relaxing bubble bath, Rosemary had chosen the substandard plumbing of this particular holiday camp – in 1995 Bognor Regis no less. There weren't even any hair dryers in the shower block and the smell of chlorine was making Joanne's eyes sting.

Joanne mused, *we could have landed in the Royal Suite at the Ritz overlooking Green Park, the hot springs of Iceland's Blue Lagoon or even the second bathroom at my parents' house in 2012. But no, Rosemary had begged to visit memories of her favourite childhood holidays.* Joanne smiled to herself, realising familiarity can bring more comfort than luxury. And the feeling of comfort was especially welcome since their run-in with the Pavilion pests.

The girls had decided to stop following Alistair and Jeremy for a while. As fun as it was to fulfil the destiny that the boys had informed them about, they agreed that they should seek out a female they admired for a change. They considered Mary Quant, Rosa Parks, Ursula Le Guin among others until Rosemary had blurted out,

"Beatrix Potter! Come on, we've visited one obliging, amiable male celebrity after another. Beatrix is known for being feisty and cantankerous, despite writing books for children. I'm intrigued as to what she was *really* like. What do you think?"

"Well, if we get chased out of her garden like Peter Rabbit looking for carrots, I'll blame you!"

"It's a deal."

"What year and what location?"

"Let me see," pondered Rosemary. "She was born in 1866 and died in 1943. By the time she was 39 she had written thirty books and was living on a farm in the Lake District."

"I love your fabulous memory," said Joanne, clearly impressed. "But I'm going to need a bit more information than that. She flipped through the book of co-ordinates in dismay.

"OK, OK," said Rosemary, tapping further into her memory. "What was the name of the farm now, *High Top*? No, that's a type of shoe. *Cliff Top*?"

"*Cliff Top*? In the *Lake District*?"

"No, no, you're right. *Hill Top*! *Hill Top Farm*. Near Sawrey. I remember reading about it now."

"Near a town called Sawrey?"

"No, *Near Sawrey* is the name of the village."

"She lived near Sawrey?"

"No, she lived *in* Near Sawrey."

"If you say so, Rosie,"

"I do say so! Try 1906. Summertime perhaps," said Rosemary with a smile. "Oh, and we should take our wings with us this time. It feels like that kind of adventure.

"Right you are. Here goes …"

The hum of the Temporal Perambulator's engine stopped almost as soon as it started. Rosemary was the first to alight, and to her delight she found that they had landed in a pretty shaded area. Patches of light peppered the ground where the sun pierced through the leaves and there was the distinct scent of summer. Her feet padded across the coolness of the mossy undergrowth. She heard the familiar sound of the Golden Knob turning in the lock above a backdrop of birdsong. Rosemary wondered how they would ever find the TP again and looked around for even a vague landmark. She spotted an oak tree, so wide that it would take three people to encircle it with arms spread wide. There was a large hollow in the base of the tree, big enough for a child to hide in, and a system of roots spread far and wide above the forest floor. A few feet away was a tree stump, surrounded by a circle of mushrooms.

"A faerie ring!" Rosemary exclaimed. "Now that's a good landmark. I won't forget that in a hurry."

"It looks like they've claimed that stump," said Joanne and hopped up onto it. She stretched out her arms and bowed low in a theatrical fashion. "I am the Queen of the Faeries!" she proclaimed in a plummy voice. "All the forest must listen to me!" Rosemary nudged her off the stump and took her place.

"No, *I'm* the Queen of the Faeries!" she declared in similar tones, only louder. "And it's hardly a forest! All the thicket must listen to me."

"Only the *thickest* will listen to you!"

Joanne nudged her back and the two of them laughed.

"Come on," said Joanne, getting her breath back. "We don't want to be looking for the TP in the dark. Which way, O Faerie Queen?"

"I propose we go that way!" said Rosemary, still in character, and began marching through the trees. A few moments later they came out onto a dusty lane. Each of them went to take a different direction.

"This way is downhill," said Rosemary, pointing down the lane. "It looks an easier route. My feet are killing me already."

"Mine are too, but see that plume of smoke up there beyond those trees? There could be a chimney or a bonfire. Either way, smoke equals civilisation."

"You're right," reasoned Rosemary.

"Besides, *Hill Top Farm* is not going to be at the bottom of a hill, is it? That would be ridiculous."

"All right, clever clogs."

"If *only* I had a pair of clogs," Rosemary sighed. "We should land in a shoe shop next time!"

The quiet lane was skirted by a partial stone wall and thriving hedgerows. There was no one around, but there were clues of inhabitants, such as a wicker basket lying on its side, apparently dropped in the middle of the lane. And a village notice board stood proudly against the tumble-down wall opposite. Joanne looked left and right, as though expecting a sudden surge of traffic in 1906, ran across the road and pored over the board's bulletins. Rosemary, meanwhile, peeked inside the basket but, alas, it was empty.

"Horse manure for sale ... lost dog ... church fundraiser ... fresh farm eggs for sale ... summer fete ..."

"How quaint," said Rosemary. "Such an idyllic place."

"Oh *please*; you'd be bored here after a weekend, city girl," scoffed Joanne.

"You're probably right," she laughed. "Let's keep going. It looks like there are some buildings ahead. Someone might be about and we can ask for directions."

The road came to an intersection with three other lanes which appeared to comprise a village centre of sorts. It was a pretty village and Rosemary could see why Beatrix, having made her fortune, had chosen to live there. A signpost that had seen better days pointed out the directions of Hawkshead (the direction from which they had come), Stoney Lane and Far Sawrey.

A cosy tavern bearing the name of Tower Bank Arms stood at the intersection. Rosemary tapped Joanne's arm in excitement as she spotted the building which was almost opposite from the tavern.

"Anvil Cottage! From *The Tale of Samuel Whiskers*!" she enthused. "So that must mean that we're not far from Farmer Potatoes' Farm!"

"Aren't we supposed to be looking for Hill Top Farm?" asked Joanne, confused.

"Yes of course. Farmer Potatoes is fictional. His farm was on Stoney Lane. Oh, this is wonderful. It's like stepping inside one of Potter's actual stories."

"A perfect little world, eh?"

"Not so perfect, really. Her writing didn't shy from reality, you know. She had animals chasing other animals and angry farmers galore. Come to think of it, Farmer Potatoes *was* based on a real-life person that Beatrix disagreed with. She got some kind of revenge on him by writing about all the rats in her story going to live in his barn, haha."

"I wouldn't mind that kind of revenge. I like rats," said Joanne with a shrug.

"And that building over there," Rosemary continued. "That's Meadow Croft, the village shop, where *Ginger and Pickles* is set."

"How about the pub?" Joanne asked, gesticulating towards the Tower Bank Arms. "Do Peter and his pals go there in *Peter Rabbit gets Hammered*?"

"You may laugh, Jo, but this is part of my childhood. I *loved* these books as a kid."

"I'm only teasing," said Joanne with a smile.

"And actually, if it hadn't been for Beatrix Potter, I probably wouldn't have read Enid Blyton's *The Adventures of Pip the Pixie*, and consequently gone on to read more grown-up fantasy novels. And then I probably wouldn't have gone to conventions or met you. So, it's all Potter's fault really."

"Ah, so *Peter Rabbit* was your gateway novel?"

"In a sense, yes. And actually, the pub *does* feature in at least one of Potter's books. I recognise it from *Jemima Puddleduck*."

Joanne remained silent, stunned by her friend's knowledge and detailed memory of her favourite childhood books and the world in which they inhabited.

Rosemary peered through the dark windows of the tavern, and before she knew it, Joanne was questioning one of the villagers. The villager, a young woman with two infants at her side, regarded the girls' appearance with a raised eyebrow. The youngsters giggled behind Granny Smith apples, possibly fresh from Meadow Croft. The mother pointed to a gate a few metres away and Rosemary saw that it was indeed the entrance to Hill Top Farm.

"I wouldn't go bothering the writer, if I were you," the woman warned. "She's a cantankerous sort. You wouldn't think such sweet little stories would come from the pen of a person so sour. My, she's even chased my boys down the street on more than one occasion. And all they did was dare to admire her garden."

Rosemary eyed the boys, whose cheeky expressions suggested that there was more to the story.

"Right, well thank you for the advice," said Joanne and the family went on their way.

"I'm not put off by that," Rosemary scoffed. "I'm not expecting her to be an angel or anything. Just meeting her would be good enough for me. Of course, an autograph would be a bonus!"

Joanne was already opening the gate, which was not locked. Rosemary followed and they passed a few hedges and borders until they spotted someone. She was sitting on a chair, facing away from them and apparently busy with something, looking up at the seventeenth-century farmhouse in front of her and down again. She did this multiple times. The most remarkable thing about the image was the fact that the woman appeared to have a huge rhubarb leaf balanced on the top of her head.

"I wonder if she knows it's there?" whispered Joanne.

"It seems to be providing a great deal of shade," said Rosemary wiping her brow with the back of her hand. "I wonder if she has any more."

The woman turned around so quickly that the leaf almost fell off. "Hey, what are you doing on my property?"

"I ... I'm so sorry, Miss Potter," Rosemary stammered. "I really like your work and I just wanted to meet you."

"Well, I'm very busy," said Beatrix and turned away again. She lifted a hand as though dismissing them, but the girls ventured nearer. Rosemary saw that Beatrix was drawing a picture of the house. It was a delicate depiction with a great deal of detail.

"Ooh I love your drawing," cooed Rosemary. "You're very talented. In all your books – I know you do all the pictures yourself."

"It's no secret," said the writer, without looking up.

"Please," said Joanne. "My friend just wants your autograph and then we will leave you to your work."

Beatrix sighed audibly, stood up and put down her pad and pencil in the deliberate fashion of someone who has been grossly inconvenienced. Beatrix looked suddenly taken aback. "Now why would you be dressed like that?" Beatrix put a hand to her chin. "Perhaps you're real fairies. Perhaps you'll be in my next book. No, no; animals are better. I like to keep fairies out of it when I can. You are an interesting pair, though. I'm not sure what to make of you. And I'm not sure what my animals would make of you. So, you'd better think about leaving." Before the girls could respond, she spoke again, mopping her brow with the huge leaf. "Well, what would you give me in return?" scowled the woman, who's scorn made her look older than her forty years.

"In ... in return for your autograph?" Rosemary stammered again. "Er ... I have some ideas for some other stories. *Peter Rabbit* is an inspiration of course, but everyone loves kittens. How about you write a tale about them? Or what about a duck? Or a mouse that lives in the countryside and a mouse that lives in the town?"

"Rose, that's enough!" Joanne admonished her, teeth clenched and eyes wide.

"Interesting. Well, if you are interested in those things, perhaps you should write about them yourself!" Beatrix scorned.

Rosemary felt something cold and heavy land on her left foot. She looked down and saw a squat frog, happily sitting there. She bent down and scooped it up. "Well, hello there, Mr Jeremy Fisher," she said and patted it gently on the head with one finger. The frog, apparently unfazed by the attention, just sat there, chest billowing in and out as it breathed. Beatrix eyed the frog and the faeries in bemusement. She appeared to be lost for words. Joanne went to pat the frog, when it leapt quickly and suddenly onto Beatrix's head, as though the leaf were a giant lily pad. The girls could not help but laugh at the absurdity and at the sudden loss of the writer's composure. The frog made one final leap and disappeared into the floral border. Beatrix threw down the leaf and glared at the pair, in a way that made them feel as though they had been sent to the headmistress's office for misbehaviour.

"Hand it over," Beatrix snapped.

"What? I don't have anything. I'm sorry," said Rosemary, still feeling like a disobedient schoolgirl.

"Your autograph book. Hand it over and I'll sign it. I would prefer you to purchase a book first, mind."

"Oh, don't worry, Miss Potter. I have them all."

"Indeed!" Beatrix scrawled in both the girls' books so quickly that it was a wonder that the signatures were legible at all. In fact, they were almost as perfectly pleasant as she was not.

"Thank you so much!" Rosemary enthused.

"I'm losing light to draw by now," said the writer with a sigh. "There's no point in me carrying on with it today. I'm going to the Tower Bank Arms for some peace."

"I'm sorry!" Rosemary exclaimed as Beatrix tidied up her things. She added "It was lovely to meet you!" because in a way, it was still an experience she would never forget.

Her response was simply a loud "Harrumph!" and a "Jeremy Fisher indeed!"

And with that she was gone.

"Did women frequent pubs in 1906?" Joanne wondered as the two of them left the beautiful farm garden, closing the gate behind them.

"She's a local celebrity. I can't see it being easy saying no to the likes of her."

"I hope you're not too disappointed," said Joanne, putting her autograph book away.

"About what?"

"About Potter turning out to be a complete sour old b—"

"Oh, it was no secret that she was a bit of a character!" Rosemary interjected. "No, I'm not disappointed at all. In fact, I'm chuffed to bits! She was quite the businesswoman as well, you know. She commissioned her own merchandise!"

"Really?"

"Yeah, even in those days it was thanks to her that there were Beatrix Potter character-themed board games, wallpaper, figurines, fabric designs, tea sets and things. She would have made a killing at ZealCon."

"Well, that's pretty inspirational. I suppose even *then* it was hard to make money just on the back of writing."

The girls made their way down the lane, back onto the dusty track, past the faerie mushroom ring and found the huge hollow tree with its sprawling roots. As dusk drew in, the girls could just make out the shiny surface of the TP, glinting through the trees.

"You know, Potter used to claim that she could see faeries. I wonder if she meant us, or just in general?" said Rosemary as Joanne unlocked the time machine.

"I don't know," replied Joanne. "But maybe you went a bit far blatantly saying *Jeremy Fisher* to that frog. Even *I* have heard of that book!"

"I know," said Rosemary, squinting her eyes in recollection. "But it just sort of ... slipped out."

"We need to be more careful. Any careless talk or action could lead to huge changes in time."

Rosemary didn't respond. She was still bathing in the afterglow of the visit which could not have been more perfect in her eyes. Beatrix had not been the most welcoming of people. But they *were* trespassing on her land. And Rosemary was accepting of almost everyone, foibles and all.

"Your turn Jo," said Rosemary, who took the opportunity to sit down. She rubbed at her aching feet.

"I've already decided where I would like to go next," said Joanne. "While we're here I thought we could drop in on Edwin Hubble. The boys went to see him after all, and we know that we end up there eventually."

"Claim Alistair and Jeremy," said Rosemary with a yawn.

"Claim the laws of physics!"

"What do you mean by, *while we're here*? Hubble was an American, wasn't he? We're in north England!"

"I meant *while we're here* in *time*, rather than geographically speaking. A young Edwin is living out his schooldays across the pond as we speak."

"Right then," agreed Rosemary. "Back to the USA we go!"

Beatrix Potter

10

"OK, here's the plan," said Joanne, bubbling with excitement. "We go and visit Edwin Hubble when he was a student at Wheaton Central High School in Chicago. We tell him we're students too; university students from Oxford! That might impress him. After all, Oxford is where Edwin ends up studying."

"Then why don't we just go straight to Oxford? Or meet him when he's older and more accomplished?" asked Rosemary with a shrug.

"Because the boys said they met him in 1906, which is when he was still at school. I do listen at astronomy club, you know."

"Sounds more like history club to me."

The Temporal Perambulator hummed through time and across the Atlantic Ocean and arrived in a narrow passageway between the sports hall and the changing rooms on a sunny day in Chicago. The girls disembarked and looked about them before attempting to navigate their surroundings. There was an unsavoury stench in the air which was coming from either a nearby dumpster or a discarded box of old trainers that Rosemary nearly tripped over. As they emerged from the passageway, a cheerleader, all cheekbones, legs and pigtails, appeared in front of them. She looked the girls up and down and sneered, "Interpretive Dance rehearsals are taking place in the drama studio, don't ya know? Not down that stinky alley." She cocked her snooty head in the air and sashayed away.

"Why are people so judgmental about the way we dress?" asked Rosemary with a sigh. "You just can't escape it, can you?"

"Story of my life. No matter what I wear. I suppose that's why we like cons so much. No one there cares. Well, mostly no one."

"Anyway, if people think we're dance students, then it can't hurt. Better than looking like a couple of twenty-something weirdos breaking into a school."

"It sounds very wrong when you put it like that!" said Joanne. "Let's avoid that cheerleading troupe and head over to that running track. It looks busy over there and someone might know where Edwin is."

"Are you sure Edwin won't be spending lunch break in Science Club or Chess – I don't know – Community or something?" asked Rosemary, confused.

"Well, I'd say it's fifty-fifty. He was a conflicted boy, was young Hubble."

"You can say that again," said Rosemary. "The sciences and P.E. couldn't be further away from each other."

"Oh, I don't know," said Joanne. "You have sports science. What about the Arts and P.E.? They're more different, I'd say."

"But then you've got the *martial arts*," said Rosemary with a grin.

"That's not the same kind of art! Anyway, I would say that religious education and the sciences would actually be the most opposing subjects."

"I'm not so sure," pondered Rosemary. "I often think that perhaps science complements some religious theory."

"We're not getting anywhere with this," said Joanne. "Come on." The girls asked pupil after pupil of the whereabouts of their next celebrity. They were about to give up and check inside the main school building when they spotted a well-built boy in shorts call after another boy in matching attire, "Ed, Ed, I bet I can beat you at the four hundred metres!"

The girls looked at each other and mouthed, "*Edwin?*"

The boy named Ed responded, "Now that I would like to see. Race you to the starting line."

But before he had chance to do so, Joanne stopped him in his tracks with a flash of her smile. The boy eyed her costume, but did not comment.

"Edwin, Edwin Hubble?"

"That's right," he replied, evidently confused by the British visitors.

"I'm Joanne and this is my friend Rosemary. Do you mind if we watch you and your friends race?"

"I guess not," he said with a smile. "Wait over there on the bleachers and I'll chat with you both after if you want."

"Great!" said Rosemary and Joanne in unison.

"*Bleachers?*" Rosemary whispered.

"I think he means those benches," said Joanne, pointing.

"Makes sense," said Rosemary and kept an eye on Edwin's position as they started to walk over.

There were other young people dotted around the benches, some actively watching the race, others just hanging around in groups and enjoying the midday sun. No one seemed too bothered by their presence. Rosemary looked on as Edwin and his competitor sprinted around the track. She realised that she was cheering him on, suddenly impressed by the young man's prowess. "Go Edwin!" she cried out. Joanne joined in and it wasn't long before others around them were joining in.

"*Now* who's the cheerleader?" laughed Joanne.

It was a close race until the final quarter where Edwin seemed to draw a final surge of energy from within himself. The burst seemed to fizzle out just as he crossed the finish line, and the girls gave a standing ovation, clapping and whooping, despite themselves. Edwin, regaining his breath, approached them.

"Well done! That was amazing!" enthused Joanne. "When you've recovered, tell us about what courses you're taking. You're quite an inspiration!"

"Oh, I'm pretty much recovered already," beamed Edwin. Rosemary felt a little uneasy as he maintained eye contact with her as he told them about himself, stretching out his muscles just inches from where they sat. She averted her eyes, aware that she might be blushing. As she turned away, she noticed the familiar forms of the other time travellers.

"Oh hello, you two," Rosemary said, hoping to cover her embarrassment. Joanne turned to them also and asked, as though they had been there all along, "have you met Edwin? He's a fantastic runner. And a brilliant basketball player too – he was just telling us all about it."

"Hi." Edwin Hubble shook their hands in turn. "Are you new to this school?"

"We're from the University of Chicago," Alistair replied. Rosemary noticed him look down at his costume. "We're visitors from the … er … drama department."

"I see," said Edwin, pulling his right foot up behind him into a quad stretch with one hand and balancing with the other. "There was nothing about it on this morning's announcements."

"The college are currently giving scholarships you know," continued Alistair, ignoring his comment. "Have you considered applying for one?"

"In sports?"

"Maybe. Or … science."

"Astronomy specifically," pushed Jeremy.

Edwin let out a huge chuckle. "And when did astronomy become classed as a science? You're more of a dreamer than I am!"

"It's interesting that you should bring the subject up, as it has been on my mind a lot lately." Edwin sat down between the two girls and fished around inside a bag which was under the bench. He pulled out a towel and mopped the perspiration off his face. "My science tutor wants to have me major in science, my math tutor wants to have me major in math and my sports coach … I just know he's going to be real disappointed if I don't take at least one sport all the way to the top. My English tutor … he would probably prefer I do any of the above – my spelling is dreadful!" He replaced the towel and pulled out a flask and took a large gulp of water.

"You certainly have a lot of options!" gasped Joanne.

Rosemary listened to the conversation with amusement. The situation felt somehow simultaneously surreal and absolutely normal. What had her life become? She felt a bit of a fraud after the Jeremy Fisher incident. And posing as ladies at the palace wasn't exactly appropriate behaviour. But a big part of her was definitely enjoying the experience of being so far out of her comfort zone.

Joanne, meanwhile, found that she was quite intrigued by Alistair. She was charmed by the fact that he was into astronomy also. Or was he just saying that he was, in order to impress Edwin? *No, that wouldn't make any sense*, she decided. He would have to have some interest in it, otherwise he wouldn't have made the effort to meet Hubble himself. He must be one of his heroes too. It seemed as though Hubble was very conflicted at this age about which path to take in his life. As she listened, she wondered whether the time travellers' presence there today was really the nudge that Edwin needed to choose to go in the direction of science and not sport? Or was time fixed and could not be changed anyway? Her head hurt just thinking about it. Edwin gave Alistair a hearty slap on the shoulder, which broke her out of her thoughts.

"You know, you're right, drama kid. I'm going to have a think about that."

A school bell pealed in the distance and the pupils started back in the direction of the school. Edwin paused. "Are you guys around later? We could go for a coffee or something. You amuse me and you seem like you'd be fun to have around."

The girls couldn't stop grinning as they made their way across the sports field and off school grounds, leaving the boys chatting to one another.

"Come on, let's see what this place has to offer," suggested Joanne. "We've got plenty of time before we meet Edwin again."

"You're not going to get another tattoo, are you?" asked Rosemary.

"Of course not. I'm still recovering from the last one. Why don't we have a look at some shoe shops, like we said before? It's not the most adventurous thing to do, but I suppose it's practical."

"I'm not knocking practical," said Rosemary, "but don't expect to find any shopping malls in 1906."

The girls wandered around for some time until they eventually came across a street which offered a bakery, a grocery store and a cobblers, but no shoe shop. Joanne eyed the row of leather shoes in the window display of the cobblers.

"Even if we found a Beatties or whatever they had in 1900 America, we don't have the dollars to pay for anything anyway."

"True," said Rosemary with a sigh. "Besides, I don't understand the foreign sizing," she added by way of attempting to convince themselves that the whole idea was fruitless. "Hey, we could always try that box of old trainers we found by the sports hall. They would be free!"

"Ugh. No thanks. I would rather go without," said Joanne and made a face. Rosemary was about to reply when she spotted an angry young man kicking a mailbox in frustration. "Hey, hey, what are you *doing*?" Joanne called out. When he looked over, she realised it was Alistair. His face softened slightly, and he approached them. "What did that mailbox ever do to you?"

"It's Jeremy. He makes me so angry sometimes. Stupid little …" and he took out his frustration further on an empty can which he kicked across the road.

"What on Earth's happened? You two seemed fine earlier."

Alistair sighed, backed towards a plain wall next to the cobblers and slumped towards the ground. The girls sat either side of him. Joanne gazed at his sullen face, his brow full of anguish and his eyes full of tears. The cocky grown man dressed as the young boot polisher had never looked so vulnerable and childlike. She shuffled closer to him and calmly waited for his reply. Alistair wiped his face with his sleeve and shrugged before he spoke.

"He just thinks he knows it all. He has this *super-brain* and he thinks he's better than me just because his sidekick is the *creator of the universe*."

"What *are* you talking about?"

"All that God stuff. He thinks he can prove to me that he exists, get his *ultimate autograph from Jesus Christ himself*, and throw it in my face."

"That doesn't sound like Jeremy," said Rosemary. "I can't imagine he would do anything malicious. Are you sure you've got it right?"

"I don't know. It's just … he gets so defensive about it all and it makes me feel like I'm in competition somehow. *I'm* supposed to be his best mate, not some invisible entity."

"I don't see why he can't have both. Even if you don't believe in Him."

"Maybe. Maybe I did overreact. But he just annoys me, you know?" Alistair seemed visibly calmer now.

"So, what happened? Did you have a fight?" asked Joanne.

"Only a full-on stand-up row in the middle of the diner. Then some jumped-up local sticks his oar in, starts having a go and making me look like Satan or something."

"A lot of Americans are very sensitive when it comes to religion."

"Well, I'm done with it!" Alistair stood up and started back down the street before the girls could say another word. He turned back briefly to them and waved, "See you later."

By the time the girls had scrambled to their feet he had turned the corner and disappeared from view. Joanne went to follow, but Rosemary stopped her.

"Maybe we should just leave him to calm down a bit more. We'll catch him later at the diner, I'm sure." Joanne nodded in agreement. Rosemary gazed absently at the shoes in the window. She could almost smell the leather. Joanne suddenly asked, "So, Rosie, what would *your* ultimate autograph be?"

"My ultimate autograph?" Rosemary didn't even have to think about it for a second. "That's easy. The person I would like to go back in time to meet would be my mother."

"That's such a brilliant idea! Why didn't I realise? Of *course* that's who you would want to meet. I'm surprised she's not the first person you wanted to rush and see, the moment we stepped into the TP!" Joanne's tongue was running away with her again.

"Well, I've been thinking about her a lot lately. During the entire trip, in fact. But I've also been so nervous about it all. I mean, what would I say to her, what would she think of me? Would I even tell her who I was? It's a bit messed up really."

"That's a good point," agreed Joanne. "You can't exactly run up to her and say, 'Hi, Mum, remember me? You knew me when I was three years old'!"

"Precisely." Rosemary sighed. "I don't know if I'd want to meet her when she had baby me at thirty-two or when she was in her early twenties or a teenager or what. Or would I just admire her from afar and get to know her that way."

"What do you know about her?"

"I remember random things about her; the way she sang, the clothes she wore and some of the things she used to say, you know? Almost as though she was on repeat; 'What the goat does, the kid follows,' 'If you do not smash an ant, it is impossible for you to find its guts.' Sometimes she would say these things in the English that you and I speak and other times she would say them in patois, 'Ef yuh nuh mash ants, yuh nuh fine im guts.' I remember that one well. I don't think I ever knew what it meant. She also sat me on her knee and told me that she was the only woman of colour in her village school, that she met Dad at uni in London, that she was really into family and our place within it and it was obvious to even toddler-me that she was utterly consumed by astronomy."

"Is that what got *you* into it to?"

Rosemary nodded. "It helps me feel close to her, in a way. It sounds cheesy when I say it out loud, but maybe she looked up at the same stars that I've looked at. Even if the actual cosmic entities we've observed through lenses no longer exist anymore."

"That makes sense," said Joanne. "Well, have a think about when and where you want to cross her timeline and let me know."

"Thanks Jo. You're a good friend."

They talked and walked a while longer and soon found themselves at the diner. The interior was nothing special, but the place was functional and clean. Joanne was disappointed that there was no music playing to add a bit of atmosphere, and the clientele were chiefly schoolchildren and twenty-somethings whose tables were littered with pastries, fries, coffee and textbooks. The aroma of coffee was prevalent, with undertones of sweat and pheromones. The girls found a booth, sat opposite each other and shuffled along to the window seats.

"Are you sure we have the right place?" asked Joanne, looking around the room. Rosemary looked towards the entrance and nodded.

"*There you are!*" Rosemary exclaimed as Jeremy and the young Edwin Hubble entered the diner. "Where's the other one?" she asked, wondering whether the two friends had yet had the chance to make up.

"Well, he was in here with me earlier," said Jeremy. "Where did you two get to?"

"Oh, just exploring," replied Joanne.

Sincerely yours
Edwin Hubble

11

The girls pocketed their autographs and made their way down the street with Jeremy who wanted to wave them off before locating the other TP and hopefully, in turn, Alistair. They turned down a side street and Joanne found a back gate into the sports field which was unlocked. They crept across the field and around to the sports hall, hoping that no one was patrolling the grounds. Rosemary was grateful that there was no such thing as CCTV in 1906. Even in America.

As they skirted around the building and into the alleyway, Rosemary now taking the lead, she came to an abrupt halt. She felt suddenly sick.

"This ... this is definitely where we landed, w... wasn't it, Jo?" she faltered. Her thoughts were such a jumble that she felt numb. She could barely make sense of what the others were saying, their vocalisations just background noise. They couldn't be stranded here. Feeling suddenly trapped, Rosemary realised that Jeremy was asking something.

"Which of you has the Golden Knob?" his voice broke through the haze of her fear. She focused on him.

"*She* does," said the girls in unison. And then, "*What?*"

"Do you mean to say that you left the key in the door?" Jeremy bit his lip.

"So, it seems," replied Joanne. "How could you forget it, Rosie? You had it at Brighton Pavilion!" she scowled at her.

"And therefore, I thought it was your turn to look after it!" Rosemary protested, the blood rushing to her face. "I can barely fit everything in my bag as it is. You know I struggled with carrying everything."

"And so you risked us getting stranded?" Joanne looked absolutely furious with her.

"*I risked it?* Why do *I* get the blame?" Rosemary was now close to tears.

"Girls, please stop the blame game," pleaded Jeremy. "Look, isn't it obvious what's happened here? Two important things have gone AWOL; that pig-headed pal of mine and the 2013 version of the TP. My guess is that the two of them must be together."

"You could be right," said Rosemary.

"You told me and Al that we had told you where we went on our travels – can you remember where we said we went next?"

Rosemary wracked her brain, willing her memory to cooperate despite the turmoil of her mind. "Er … After visiting Hubble, Alistair said that he went back to Christmas."

"*Christmas?*" Jeremy reiterated.

"I remember the strange expression on his face … as though he was mocking, jeering …"

"I think I know which Christmas Alistair was talking about," said Jeremy.

"Or *will* be talking about."

"Come on, let's go and get in the other TP."

Of course, thought Rosemary. *The other version of the TP. We're not trapped after all.*

After a few quarrels with the TP, the Gregorian calendar, and among themselves, the three of them were soon careering backwards through time, enduring the claustrophobia-inducing journey all the way back to the year 30 AD. The couple of minutes that it took certainly felt much longer.

"My body clock is all over the place," said Rosemary as they stumbled out of the TP. "I feel as though I've got jetlag. It's morning again!" All three gazed at the sunrise which dominated the landscape. They could almost smell the blaze of the orange radiance as the sun bathed the sandy plains in the newness of the day. It was truly awe inspiring. Scanning over to the east, Joanne spotted a smattering of civilisation in the form of small, simple buildings, nestled among plants and trees. A sudden warm breeze reminded the travellers that this was all very real. Joanne felt a mixture of excitement, joy and apprehension at their impending adventure. They were in a strange land where people spoke a different tongue and they would probably encounter the biggest culture gap yet. Joanne was wary about how she and Rosemary would be received as foreigners and female time foreigners at that.

"So how do you know that he's here at this point in time?" Joanne asked Jeremy, attempting to cover up her trepidation.

"Well, if we were unable to travel back to year zero, then Al would have encountered the same issue. Plus, the stable wasn't like St Thomas' hospital you know – Mary and Joseph wouldn't have been in and out in the same day."

"Maybe. If any of this is true, perhaps they stayed put for a few months," said Joanne. She peered back into the TP at the monitor which read Year 30 AD Cana, beneath the long time/location co-ordinate. "But I'm not sure about *30 years*. Jez – up until now, which of you had been operating the controls?"

"Alistair. Why do you ask?"

"Year 30 AD, *Cana*? Where on Earth is *Cana*? If we *are* still on Earth," She breathed deeply. "At least it has a breathable atmosphere."

"Cana ... why do I know that name?" Jeremy mused. "How did we end up here?"

"Maybe the machine has a life of its own!" said Joanne.

"Or maybe I just sent us on the incorrect course," Jeremy sighed. "We should get back inside."

"Ooh what's happening over there? That looks exciting!" Rosemary stepped away from the machine and pointed at a large, bustling group of people who were emerging from the west and making their way towards the group of buildings. Some were singing, others were dancing and whooping and others were carrying musical instruments that she had never seen before. It was like being in a biblical version of Birmingham Broad Street on a Saturday night. She would not have been surprised if one of them was carrying a traffic cone on their head.

"We haven't got time to find out!" Jeremy insisted.

"Haven't got *time*? Come on, Jez, we've got as much time as we need! We can go back whenever we want. And when we *do* decide to go, Joanne will set the controls for you, so you don't have to worry about taking us off course. Let's just see what's going on – it won't take long. Please."

"All right. Just for a little while."

Joanne, surprised at her friend's sudden lack of care and lust for spontaneity, shrugged and grabbed Rosemary's hand. The girls grinned at each other. Of course, they would find Alistair, but he was the one who ran off, after all. And what was an adventure without a party?

"It looks like a big celebration – a wedding perhaps," Rosemary squealed with excitement.

"Wedding celebrations in these times went on for days," Jeremy informed them. "But I'm not sure we should really be –"

But Rosemary had already grabbed hold of his hand too as they headed towards the largest of the buildings. Close up, the edifice was at least as large as a town hall. It was simple in structure and bustling with life, even as the sun came up.

The gatecrashers had barely got a metre inside the building when a bouncer of sorts jabbed a finger at each of them.

"It's our clothes, isn't it?" asked Jeremy. Rosemary stifled a laugh. The man said something in his own language. Jeremy simply looked confused and turned to the girls. "I know it's a bit of a long shot, but did either of you take an evening class in Aramaic?"

"I did," said Joanne.

"Really?" His eyes widened.

"Of course I didn't!" she laughed.

The man pointed at a row of huge stone pots, filled to the brim with what looked, and smelled, like pond water.

"You don't have any Bucks Fizz then?" Jeremy's grin disappeared when the man grabbed hold of his collar and jabbed a finger at the containers again. A guest entered the building and dipped his hands into the pot nearest to him, nonchalantly dried his hands, greeted the doorman and waltzed past them. "Oh, the pots are for *washing*," said Jeremy with relief. The man seemed satisfied once the three of them followed suit and passed through the entrance.

They had barely walked another few metres, however, when they were stopped again. A woman looked scornfully at the garments in which the travellers were dressed. She then placed a pile of heavy, woollen garments into Rosemary's arms and said, "simlāh, simlāh."

"It's like the opposite of a night club cloak room!" she whispered to Joanne.

Rosemary distributed the suspect-smelling material among the three of them.

"You look as though you had an argument with a tumble-dryer and lost," laughed Joanne, who got along with material much better than her friends.

"How do you do that without a mirror?" Jeremy asked.

"Practice," Joanne shrugged.

"You like dressing up don't you, *Sir Cuthbert?*" Rosemary asked Jeremy with a smile.

"Of course, but I generally only wear one costume at once." He tapped the heels of his winkle-pickers together for good measure.

"Come on," said Rosemary. "I can smell food."

The girls did not notice that Jeremy wasn't with them until it was too late.

Where's he got to now? Joanne wondered. She spotted a jumble of tables, swathed in cloth. Upon the cloth sat bowl after bowl of all manner of food. Joanne helped herself to some grapes and Rosemary took a hunk of warm bread and they smiled at each other, chewing away.

"I love grapes too, but I prefer the fermented kind," said Joanne with a wink and looked around her at people who had goblets in their hands. Some of them were grumbling and seemed to be complaining that their goblets were dry. "Oh dear. I wonder where the bar is?"

"I think it *was* over there," Rosemary said, pointing at a disgruntled group of people gathered around some large stone water jars. One man drained his cup and the man next to him snatched it from his hand, elbowed him in the ribs and snarled at him. Another shouted out and stumbled into one of the jars, causing it to sway unsteadily. The ruckus did not escalate any more than that, but it was still quite an alarming sight. Rosemary spotted Jeremy in the crowd and spun him around.

"There's no wine left!" Rosemary complained and pointed at the scuffle.

"I thought you were looking for food," said Jeremy.

Joanne sighed. "Whoever heard of a free bar that ran dry?"

"Quite a lot of people as it happens …" said Jeremy.

"Well maybe in your circles, but it's considered very rude where I come from." Joanne was half joking, but Jeremy looked as though he was taking her seriously.

"Look, I'm sure it's considered very rude here too and, if I know my history, the bride and bridegroom would be pretty embarrassed if they had run out of celebratory wine," said Jeremy. "Which makes me think …"

"What?" asked Rosemary.

"Ssh," he held up a hand, still serious. "Could it really be?" He turned to where the commotion had taken place. Where had the bearded man and the servants gone? "I need to find that man!"

"What man?" Joanne asked. "You mean – do you think you've found him? *Here?*"

"Let me put it this way – if it is who I think it is then you don't need to worry about the wine situation!" As the words came out of his mouth, a company of men entered the room carrying more stone water jars between them. It was apparent that water was sloshing over the top and onto the dusty floor below. The jars must have held twenty or thirty gallons each. They set them down. There was much gesticulating of arms and pointing at those jars and the ones which had held the wine which were different.

"I think those are ritual jars of some sort, like the ones we washed our hands in," Joanne whispered. "Those people don't seem very pleased!" An important-looking man advanced towards the jars, people standing aside for him. He took his goblet, dipped it into one of the jars and sipped it. He nodded, held his goblet aloft and made some kind of positive declaration. Joanne, Rosemary and Jeremy looked at each other. The man called someone over who looked as though he might be the bridegroom from the way that he was dressed and his body adorned. The man smiled and declared something to him before the whole room erupted in cheers and song.

"What did he say?" Rosemary asked.

"If I can remember my Bible, he said something about most people serving the good wine first until people are sufficiently drunk and then the poor wine. But today, the good wine has been kept until now. The water has been turned into wine! I *knew* it was Jesus and his mother I saw talking earlier. I can't believe it!"

"Nothing has changed much then," said Joanne with a laugh. "Everyone at a party drinks the good wine and beer first then goes onto the dregs and dodgy bottle of twenty-twenty from the back of the cupboard."

"*That's what you're taking from this?*" asked Jeremy, shaking his head. "You just witnessed a miracle, Joanne!"

"Not really," said Joanne. "I saw a man drink some wine that those guys brought in and everyone is happy again." Jeremy sighed. Rosemary saw his frustration and wondered whether he felt resigned to the fact that there was little chance of them sharing his joy.

Rosemary put a hand on his shoulder and said honestly to him, "It *did* look like they were filled with water before. And he definitely has wine on his chin now." She smiled at him and he smiled back. She opened her mouth to speak again but Joanne had grabbed hold of her hand and began dancing with her. She felt she had little choice in the matter and got herself caught up in the festive atmosphere. They danced until their feet grew sore, not least from people stepping on their bare toes. And they sang until their throats became hoarse, despite not knowing any of the words. Rosemary was aware of Jeremy not being around for a while and then appearing again a little while later, with his usual worried look on his face. For a man with such a great sense of humour, he really needed to relax sometimes and let himself smile thought Rosemary.

"I think we need to think about leaving," said Jeremy, shouting above the music. "I've failed in my mission and I'm getting really worried about – "

"– Alistair yeah," said Rosemary. "I've been thinking about him too. I think I'm starting to miss him. Or maybe it's just the effect of the wine. It's *very* good wine …"

"So I see."

"Come on then Jez," Rosemary said, putting an arm around his shoulder, partly in an effort to steady herself and partly to feel close to him. Joanne put an arm playfully around his other shoulder. They noticed that they were receiving some very strange glances from the wedding guests.

"Er ... it's *definitely* time to leave," said Jeremy, apparently feeling threatened.

"Fine, fine," said Joanne, casually and they battled their way through the crowds and out into the cool evening air.

"It was just getting started though," said Joanne. "But that's OK because we left before we got too carried away and anything too crazy happened. I think we managed to stay inconspicu ... inconspishucu ... spinconcnistu ..."

Jeremy said nothing, but Rosemary started to giggle uncontrollably at her friend. Jeremy's demeanour cracked and his eyes twinkled with mirth.

When they reached the Temporal Perambulator, Jeremy helped the girls inside. They found their footing, holding onto the interior of the TP for balance. Before Jeremy could shut the door, however, a sudden unexpected deep, hoarse moan echoed through the air.

There came an anguished cry, "JEZEBEL!"

12

Jeremy slammed the door in apparent fear. He stared at the girls, wide-eyed in the blinking lights of the tiny TP. Rosemary remarked that it looked as though he had seen a ghost.

"You're not far off," Jeremy gulped. "It was moaning and groaning and well ... It was saying *Jezebel*."

"Isn't that what Al calls you?" asked Joanne. She stifled a hiccup which got caught in her chest. She tried to appear sober and logical. "What's he doing here?"

"Well, he's obviously looking for you," Rosemary told Jeremy. They were almost two thousand years into the past. They couldn't very well leave him there, no matter what state he was in, she reasoned.

"What are we doing, faffing about in here? We'll go and get him," stated Joanne.

Jeremy explained that in the brief glimpse he had had of him, Alistair had appeared to be limping and covered in bandages. A terrifying vision. "He was lolling along like some kind of zombie mummy creature ..."

Rosemary and Joanne shared a look.

There was a sudden, loud clanging on the door followed by muffled moaning and more clanging. Jeremy tentatively opened the TP door and Alistair fell into the time-machine.

"Finally!" Joanne remarked and took to the controls.

"No!" Alistair cried, his mummified hand suddenly on hers.

"It's OK; I've not had that much to drink, Alishter. Besides, I haven't even got a driving licence to lose. And there's the fact that this isn't even a *car* – "

"It's nothing to do with you being at the controls," Alistair protested. He looked into her eyes. Joanne had never seen him look so serious. "You can't take me – not *this* version of me."

"What do you mean?" asked Jeremy.

Alistair took a deep breath and explained. "I've come to ask you all to go and rescue me. I was mugged near the river Jordan – they took my wallet, my phone and the Golden Knob. A charitable couple looked after me for a day or two and then you and the girls turned up at the house and returned my things so that I was no longer trapped there."

"How did we know to do that?" asked Rosemary, confused.

"Because I'm telling you now. I've come here to tell you to go back – well, forward – to the bandit camp north of the river to retrieve my things, then come and find me at the couple's house."

"Why can't we just go back – *forward* – and stop the thieves in their tracks? Get to them first, before they get to you?" asked Rosemary.

"Because that's not what happened," said Alistair, desperately.

"I need another drink," said Joanne. "I don't normally have any problem with following *Sir Cuthbert's Remarkable Adventurers Through Time*, but when it's real …"

"… you start to doubt logic," finished Rosemary. "It's important that we do this right."

"So how did you get here again?" asked Joanne.

"In the TP, I presume, after we gave him back the Golden Knob. Correction – *the Golden Knob he stole in the first place*."

Alistair gave an apologetic smile.

"Yeah … I'm sorry about that Jez. But I was trying to make it up to you … I was trying to get the dude's autograph for you. I was right there at the river where He was baptised!"

"Or trying to prove me wrong, maybe?" It was obvious that Jeremy had still not forgiven Alistair.

"Please don't get into all this again now, boys," Joanne begged.

"And yes, you're right about the TP. I got here in *our* TP, Jez. A not-so-cross future version of you is waiting for me in it right now so I'd better go before he *does* get cross."

"All right. Al, can you explain in as much detail as possible how we can find this bandit camp so that we can get your things back?"

Rosemary turned to Joanne and whispered, "Do you remember that *Sir Cuthbert's Remarkable Adventures Through Time* story where his companion had an adventure which was parallel to his? The following episode was the same adventure from the companion's point of view, but half of the scenes were duplicated from the first episode and just shown from a different camera angle?"

"I remember that," Joanne replied. "Series 3 two-parter Christmas special: 'A Proper English Escapade.' It was a good story, but they didn't need all the duplication in the second episode, especially as most viewers had seen episode one anyway. They didn't quite strike the right balance between new material and the POV element …"

"That's what I was thinking about too," mused Rosemary. "And they broke the fourth wall a few times in that story too. Most odd."

Joanne looked up and winked.

"What are you doing?" Rosemary asked.

"Oh, don't worry about it."

"When are you going next?" asked Jeremy when he finally dropped two tired faeries back at their own TP.

"I'm sure you'll bump into us again," said Joanne.

"You two really are frustratingly annoying sometimes, you know," said Jeremy. "Or annoyingly frustrating. Both."

"Yes, we know," said Rosemary.

"Thanks for helping me rescue Al, anyway. I don't think I would have wanted to face those bandits on my own."

"I'm sure you'll repay the favour," said Joanne. She closed the door and took to the controls. The time machine started to glow and hum into life.

"You don't always have to be so enigmatic around them," noted Rosemary.

"Why not?" Joanne asked with a laugh. "It's fun! The look on their faces when we're one step ahead of them is hilarious."

"True," agreed Rosemary. "Let's have some more fun."

"We could," said Joanne. "But I have a feeling you're just trying to delay proceedings."

"What do you mean?"

"Don't you want to visit your mum?"

"Of course I do. The opportunity is right here, Jo – it's dangling in front of me like a … a … Oh, I don't know … overwhelming, unpredictable … thing! I'm too scared. Apprehensive maybe. I don't feel like going to see her just yet. Do you mind?" She turned to Joanne.

"Of course not." Joanne didn't push the matter any further.

"Besides," said Rosemary, "it's your turn to choose. I chose Hubble. Whose autograph do *you* want next?"

Joanne paused, thought for a moment and then smiled, as though someone had lit a sparkler insider her head. "We've met royalty, we've met an astronomer, we've met actors and a writer. But we haven't yet met any famous fashion designers."

"And fashion's your thing!" exclaimed Rosemary.

"After a fashion," said Joanne with a smile. "Let's face it, I have never been one to bother to keep up with the latest trends. But I love my costumes and beautiful fabric and style and ideas and …"

"So, who are you thinking about?" Rosemary asked, excitedly. "Tell me!"

"Well, I have always wanted to meet Vivienne Westwood."

"Well, she certainly had lots of original ideas."

"Exactly. And I *love* the punk era."

"I always thought she might be a bit ... scary though."

"Don't worry." Joanne reassured her. "I'll protect you!"

"She's still alive, isn't she?"

"Well, technically she's not born yet." Joanne jabbed a finger in the direction of the door, referring to the biblical times in which they still stood.

"All right, smart-arse. By those terms, neither are we! I was talking about in our own time. In 2012 she's not a historical figure or anything."

"Yeah. She's got to be in her seventies. But I want to meet her during the thick of it – when she was young and feisty and in the midst of all the controversy."

"Sounds like it could be fun," said Rosemary. "Let's go!"

The TP landed near Fetter Lane Moravian Church, Chelsea. There was no one around when Joanne popped her head out of the door. Rosemary followed her out of the side street and onto Millman Street and then out onto the busy Kings Road.

"London, I take it?" Rosemary asked as they walked along the tarmac.

"Yes, but I think we've arrived a bit early. The address of the shop where Vivienne and Malcolm McLaren worked is 430 King's Road. But it looks like we're still in the sixties."

"How do you know the exact address?"

"It's a very famous shop; Sex! It's pretty much where the punk scene started, Rosie! I thought you liked the Sex Pistols and stuff like that?"

"I like a bit of everything really. Sorry for not knowing all the details," Rosemary huffed. She admitted that the people around them certainly seemed to be dressed in sixties-era styles. The younger people, at least, looked like they had stepped out of a vintage magazine. And they were in Chelsea after all. And the older people looked much older than they probably were. A lady with short hair, oversized glasses and a long overcoat looked at first glance to be a pensioner, but she was probably actually no older than Joanne's mum. She gazed across the street. "Look at that shop front." Rosemary pointed across the road at a narrow shop with the lettering "Hung on You" brightly painted on the window. The glass was embellished with colourful motifs and stood out from the rest of the street. It was an intriguing vision. "What is it, I wonder? A café, a market?"

"It's funny you should ask that because *that's* 430 King's Road. It used to be all sorts of things before it was the famous Sex. We might be in the wrong time, but we are definitely in the right place."

"Sex seems like an outrageous name for a shop. Even now," mused Rosemary.

The girls crossed the road with ease as there was not much traffic about. Rosemary peered through the window. "It looks like a greengrocers or something. I don't think we need any apples. Shall we travel to the right time?"

"Yes all right, let's head to the seventies. As much as I *love* this era!" Joanne was so distracted by a woman dressed head to toe in hippy-chic that she almost got run over on their way back across Kings Road.

"Watch where you're going!" Rosemary shrieked. "I'm not lugging your dead body back to the twenty-first century."

"I'm fine, I'm fine," said Joanne dismissively as they ambled back down Millman Street.

Joanne manipulated the TP's controls in an attempt to reach the correct time co-ordinates. When they next stepped out onto Kings Road, spring was in the air and the street was markedly busier. There was a motorbike parked outside number 430 and a group of youngsters were going inside. The shop was still not called Sex, however, but Let It Rock. It had a completely different feel about it to the 1960s version. The large, blocky writing was proudly emblazoned across a corrugated sheet above the shop window. Rosemary thought it looked a bit like the entrance to a night club. Although they were still not in the right time, the girls agreed to go inside anyway. One of the youngsters was talking to another. "I don't know, Mike. I really liked it when it was Paradise Garage. All that Americana is kinda cool. I'm not sure about this Teddy Boy fashion. It all seems a bit old hat. Like something my dad would wear."

"We don't come here for the fashion, Andy – I leave all that stuff to my girl. We come here for the Aladdin's Cave that is the back room." The second boy beckoned the first through the small shop and into a back room and Rosemary and Joanne followed. What confronted them was somewhat of a surprise. Instead of the dingy afterthought of a back room they were expecting, they were greeted by what looked like a lively retro living room with fitting ornaments and armchairs to boot.

"This is wonderful!" Joanne exclaimed. "It's even cooler than I thought. It looks like a film set."

"Is this their home?" Rosemary asked, confused. "Vivienne and Malcolm's, I mean."

"No, no, it's a record shop. Just look around you!"

Sure enough, among the Teddy Boy paraphernalia, drape jackets and quiffs, were boxes of vinyl records which the youngsters were poring over.

"You're into your fashion so you're the right person to ask," said Rosemary. "Why on Earth were they called Teddy Boys?"

"Ted comes from *Edwardian*. They liked to wear 1900s clothes and called themselves Teds."

"I see," pondered Rosemary. "I always associate the look with my dad's brother Steve with his mouldy old jacket, greasy slicked-back hair and fag hanging out of his mouth. I didn't realise that people actually looked cool back then."

Joanne laughed. "I'm sure, in his head, he still looks like this."

"I'm sure I'll respect him a bit more now. When he's not coughing all over me and swearing his head off, maybe."

"Can I help you?" A woman of about thirty years old was crossing the room, arms full of fabric.

"Are you Dame Westwood?" Joanne asked then bit her tongue.

"*Dame?*" the woman laughed and dumped the fabric on the counter. "I should think not. I'm Vivienne Westwood though."

"What are you going to make with those?" Rosemary asked, her hand unconsciously feeling the fabric. She was very tactile when it came to material and she struggled to prevent herself from stroking clothes, even when people were wearing them, because she just had to know how they felt: soft, rough, warm, cool, fluffy.

"Something for Malcolm I expect. He wants me to make some Ted clothes like the ones in the front. But I might make him something a bit different. I don't know yet." The slim woman with the striking blonde hair stopped a moment to take in the scene before her and regarded the girls. "Do you two dress alike often?" It was hard to know whether she was being judgemental, but Vivienne certainly seemed intrigued by them.

"We're cosplayers," blurted Rosemary.

"You've lost me. You're players? Actors?"

"Sort of," said Joanne. "We make our own costumes."

"Or buy them and add bits together to make them our own," added Rosemary. "We emulate characters or create our own characters."

"I see," said Vivienne. "And what do you call this look?"

"We're just fairies," said Rosemary, proudly.

"Very creative. I like it. It's fun, at least."

"Thank you! Thank you so much!" Joanne's enthusiasm for her idol validating her sewing skills was almost too much and Vivienne looked taken aback.

"Right. Well, is there anything you'd like to buy?"

"Oh, we don't own record players," said Rosemary, glumly. "But we'll look around. It's a fantastic place."

"Browsing is free," said Vivienne.

"There is one thing though," said Joanne and fumbled around for her autograph book, her nervousness making her hands shake. However, a man with wild red hair appeared by the fashion designer's side and drew her attention away. When Joanne looked up, she was gone.

"Why didn't you stop her?" Joanne implored.

"Sorry I was looking over there at those things," she waved an arm in the direction of a wall display. "Anyway, I couldn't really have stopped them, could I? They're busy people."

"Can I help you?" Another woman appeared at the counter. Joanne shook her head and marched out of the shop, Rosemary at her heel.

"I was *so* nervous then. And she said she liked my sewing! I can't believe that we lost her."

"Well come back in the shop and wait five minutes then. I'm sure they won't be long. Don't be daft."

"No. I want to go a bit further forward than a few minutes. The punk era is where it's at." Joanne was walking so quickly that Rosemary struggled to keep up. She just hoped she had calmed down by the time they returned to the TP.

13

Joanne delighted in explaining to Rosemary that it must be 1974 because they had now arrived at the shop just as the hard rock-style Too Fast To Live, Too Young To Die sign was coming down and the bright, pink plastic padded Sex lettering was going up. She looked exceedingly pleased with herself.

"I couldn't have timed it more perfectly," she boasted.

"It only took you three goes!" Rosemary reminded her.

"And *this time* we get to see two frontages at once."

"I'm sorry, I didn't realise we were going on a tour of shop frontages. We're supposed to be collecting autographs. I'll never meet my mum at this rate."

"You're the one who wanted to procrastinate!"

"Yes, OK, you're right. And it *is* kind of interesting. But we're going to look *really* out of place here; faerie dresses and punk rock?"

"Punk rock is not a fashion statement, it's a state of mind, Rosie."

"Says the wannabe fashion designer."

"Oh, just come on, will you?" Joanne led the way across the road once more and into Sex. An older couple crossed the road away from the shop in a purposeful manner, muttering something about the "state of the world today" and tutting at the new blatant signage. Inside the shop, a transition stage of sorts was evident, with drain-pipe jeans, leather, ruffle shirts and boots on one wall and more outrageous styles of a fetish nature hung on racks which were taking up substantial floorspace. Rosemary looked with wonder at the intrepid feminist quotes which were scrawled across thick latex-covered walls and took in the bold atmosphere. A young woman was re-arranging some of the clothing and chatting with a customer. She had very short, bleached blonde-hair, dark eye makeup and wore revealing PVC clothing and spiked heels. She looked comfortable in herself and happy in her work.

"Thanks Jordan, see you next week no doubt," the customer said and exited the shop, hands full of shopping bags.

"That must be *the* Jordan," Joanne whispered to Rosemary. "She was in all sorts of cool movies and documentaries in the late seventies. She was also Adam and the Ants' manager."

"Maybe we should get her autograph too!" gushed Rosemary.

"That might seem a bit odd. She's just a shop girl at this point!"

"How do you know all this stuff?"

"When I research fashion I often get stuck down rabbit warrens of information. It's interesting though, eh?"

"No need to be shy, girls!" Jordan hung a leather-studded item on its hanger and faced them. "Have a look around!"

"Thanks," said Joanne. "We were just wondering if Dame ... I mean *Miss* Westwood, is in today."

"She's not in at the –" At that moment, the shop door burst open and in danced Vivienne, as though onto a stage.

"I have the perfect idea for a new line, Jordan – I'll tell you about it over lunch," said Vivienne, enthusiastically. "Oh, hello girls." She eyed them for a couple of seconds. "I recognise that style – *faerie chic*." The girls looked at each other. Neither of them knew what to say. Vivienne continued. "And it seems like the style is back for the summer. Fabulous. It went quite well with the whole flower power thing, but I suppose you could embellish it. Here."

The fashion designer sourced a leather waistcoat from a rail and hung it over Joanne's shoulders. She shook her head, replaced it on the hanger and strode across the room. She plucked something from a box, opened the packaging and a pair of black fish-net tights concertinaed out. Vivienne looked at Joanne for a moment then back at the tights and ripped a large hole in one leg. She handed them to Joanne and nodded at her. "Well, go on then. It's all right, there's no charge. I should pay *you* for acting as my mannequin for a minute."

"OK," said Joanne and tentatively put on what was left of the tights, there in the middle of the shop. A customer dressed head to toe in studded leather trudged into the shop in a big pair of bovver boots. He paid the girls no mind and started browsing. Vivienne put her hands on her hips and smiled. She turned to Rosemary and then squinted, looked around the shop. She picked up a PVC belt from a rack and handed it to her and Rosemary knew what to do.

"Put some leather ribbons in your hair and the look would be complete!" Vivienne said with a reserved smile. She was evidently very pleased with her mish-mash creation. "You two could be in a band."

"Oh, I can't sing," both said, in unison.

"Right, never mind," Vivienne said, almost disappointed. "Is there anything else I can get you?"

"Do you sell shoes?" asked Rosemary, before remembering that they had no current currency. Vivienne went to respond when Joanne interjected, "Please could we have your autograph? It would make our day!"

"Of course," said Vivienne. Grinning, the girls held out their books.

"You're such an inspiration," bleated Joanne as she watched the ink make its way across the page. "I am *definitely* going to study fashion. I should enrol on a course this autumn." To her surprise, Vivienne's face fell.

"What else are you interested in?"

"Er … astronomy."

"Do that; don't do fashion." Vivienne shook her head.

"But —"

"Believe me. You seem like a sweet girl. The fashion industry will poison your blood. It will eat you alive. Express yourself in your own way, but if you've got the brains, then stick to astronomy."

"Right." Joanne didn't know what to say to that. She looked at Rosemary who shrugged, and then back at her idol.

"Do you have these in a thirty-two-inch waist?" the customer called across the shop. Vivienne smiled at the girls then went to see to him. Joanne stared after her. Her heart felt heavy, as though it was being weighed down. She had felt as light as air only a few moments ago. Vivienne had made her feel so special. She would have gladly given up everything to be her mannequin. And now she felt let down and melancholy enveloped her.

"How could she say that to me?" Joanne asked as they walked back to the TP. "Vivienne, my wonderful Vivienne told me to give up on my dreams!"

"Not because you're no good," said Rosemary. "She was trying to protect you! It's tough out there — even *tougher* in 2012. She knows that and she's looking out for you."

"Then she's a hypocrite — because look at this shop and all of her creations and think of how big her empire is now! How *dare* she stamp on my dream." There were tears in her eyes. Rosemary didn't know what to say. She knew how much fashion meant to Joanne and nothing she could think of to say seemed enough.

"Come on," sighed Rosemary. "Let's go and get something to eat somewhere."

14

Joanne and Rosemary were eating fish and chips with curry sauce in a small fish bar in 2012 London. Both were hungrier than they had realised and were so contented by their consumption that they didn't speak for a full fifteen minutes. Once she had finished her portion, Joanne rolled up the empty greasy wrapper into a ball, set it aside, took a long swig of cola and let out a loud belch. She covered her mouth, suddenly embarrassed, and looked around. No one seemed fazed, apart from Rosemary, who shook her head and took a sip of her own drink.

Rosemary found comfort in doing such a normal activity in her hometown in her real time. The sounds, smells, sights were all so familiar. The music blasting from the tinny fish bar stereo was music from the 90s and 00s, the cars parked outside were recognisable and people were dressed in modern apparel. Apart from Rosemary and Joanne of course. It had become a running joke between them now. They had chosen to dismiss the idea of shopping for shoes, everyday clothing or even coats to wear over their costumes, on their ultimate quest for autographs – like an endurance test. Rosemary felt quite at home in the melting-pot of London. Even this small fish bar was frequented by people of all ethnicities. Having grown up in London and feeling so grounded there, it often felt like a slap in the face when anyone should suggest otherwise. She may have felt out of her time in the 1970s, 1950s and during the biblical times. But this was *her* time and *her* city, and she was enjoying being back there for a short while before they continued their adventures. So when a group of young lads came in and started swearing at a Polish man who had just ordered chips for his family and then their frontman turned to face her, his face full of malice and hatred, Rosemary remembered why sometimes she hated living in the city. If it could be hard for her, it must have been really difficult for her mother.

"Oh, go and find your other braincell, will you?" Joanne shouted at the lads and threw her balled-up chip wrapper at the main perpetrator.

"What's it got to do with you?" he spat.

"A hate crime is a hate crime, and it affects everyone. We were just trying to enjoy our dinner. But now the place is full of *undesirables*!" Joanne got to her feet and headed towards the door, shooting a look at Rosemary.

"*We're* the undesirables?" another lad shouted. "Look around you. You're one of us!"

Joanne looked them up and down. "I'll never be like you." Heart running a marathon in her chest, she held the door open for Rosemary and both walked swiftly down the street, hoping that they would not be followed.

"Thanks for that. But I can fight my own battles," Rosemary said, once they were clear of the fish bar and anonymous among the crowds again.

"It's not just your battle," said Joanne with a sigh. "Haters need to learn. I had enough of it in school, being called a boffin and a geek. Even though I embrace the term *geek* now."

"It's hardly the same."

"I know. But the scars are still there."

Rosemary gave her friend's hand a squeeze and they made their way back to the TP, which they had parked in an alley way off Leicester Square.

"It's times like this that my mum would talk about Mary Seacole," said Rosemary as they stepped into the solace of the TP. "She would talk about how she was a strong

British-Jamaican woman and how proud she was of being one too and how proud she was of me."

"It sounds like she had a really positive impact on you," said Joanne, who located the book of co-ordinates. "She obviously encouraged you a lot."

"She did. It's just a shame she's not still around. I could have done with her encouragement in my teens. Dad was great, but – "

"– but a girl needs her mum."

"Exactly." Rosemary noticed Joanne thumbing through the book and scrutinising its pages. "Jo, what are you doing?"

Joanne put the book away, turned to the console and tapped and dialed in a pattern of co-ordinates. The Temporal Perambulator hummed into life and Rosemary asked the question again.

"What did it look like I was doing? I was programming the TP. Let's grab some sunscreen. We're off to Jamaica!"

It transpired that the sunscreen wasn't needed, however, as they appeared to arrive during Jamaica's wet season. Joanne poked her head out of the TP and turned back to Rosemary, her bouncy blonde curls plastered to the sides of her face in a matter of seconds. Rosemary guffawed with laughter.

"Maybe we can find one of those women who offer to braid hair for tourists?" she said with a smile.

"In the early 1800s? Anyway, even if we had the dollars, we don't have the time."

Then, suddenly, it was as though someone had flicked a switch to make the rain stop. Bright yellow light bled through pale clouds which then quickly scattered themselves across the blue sky until they had almost completely dissolved. The warmth of the sun wrapped them both in a comforting hug.

"That's Jamaica, for you!" said Rosemary.

"Have you been here before, by the way?" asked Joanne as she locked the TP and scanned their surroundings.

"I've been to Montego Bay," replied Rosemary. "Although I always wanted to go to Kingston. I don't know why we never did, considering our family history."

"Did you go with your mum and dad?"

"My dad, cousins, and aunt and uncle. We stayed in the resort, mostly. My dad's not that adventurous."

"You must have got your adventurous side from your mum, then."

Rosemary shrugged and asked, "So at what point in Mary's life have we arrived at then? She travelled backwards and forwards between here and London for a big chunk of her life, so we might have more chance of bumping into her in the middle of the ocean!"

"I don't know that much of her history, to be honest, considering how big a deal she is to historians now. Maybe we could just speak to some locals and find out?"

"That's incredibly vague!" Rosemary protested. "Needle and haystack come to mind. Oh, why didn't I press my mum for more info on her? Or we could travel to a library and do a quick Google?"

"Now, where's the fun in that?"

Rosemary lifted her arms, exasperated, as she followed her friend to who-knew-where-next. Rosemary was no historian either, but she knew that during this time many black people were forced into enslavement. She was also aware that the Seacoles lived in a community of "free people" and that Mary's mother was from Jamaica and her father from Scotland. Rosemary felt a mixture of emotions as they walked inland from where they had parked the TP. Even if they had landed in the middle of a safe community, she still felt a little uneasy. She felt proud to be here, but also wary. Wary was often Rosemary's default state, wherever she happened to be. She just didn't always show it. Joanne, however, was boldly marching on, oblivious to any glances from locals. Rosemary wondered whether

Joanne had actually had a plan all along. Rosemary questioned her.

"OK, you've got me," she said and halted. "While we were in the fish bar, I used their WiFi to do a bit of research."

"Now where's the fun in that?" Rosemary mocked her, laughing. "OK, so where are we going? Ugh, I feel like I've swallowed a broken record."

"That makes no sense."

"I don't care. I'm not asking again."

"OK," Joanne sighed. "We're going to Blundell Hall, where Mary and her siblings grew up. It was a lodging house owned by her mother. It's where she observed some of her mother's nursing skills. Although Mary was officially the first nurse practitioner, her mother was a kind of healer."

"OK. How far away is this Hall?"

They were interrupted by the shrill voice of a panicked parent in patois, "Louisa, nuh mek mi call yuh again. Yuh cum an join yuh sistah and bredda fi dinna rite dis instant." A barefoot child swept past them. On arriving at Blundell Hall, a large structure which loomed before them, the child planted her hands on her hips and said, "Buh ma, Mary a still rampin wid har dolls!" Louisa pointed at another little girl of about twelve, sitting on the step and wrapping a bandage around the arm of a rag doll.

"Nuh yuh worry bout dat. Yuh jus worry bout yuhself. Shi hav bin learning all day," the mother retorted, "Git yuhself inna. Mary, yuh too now."

Both girls followed their mother inside and the door closed behind them.

"I think we've arrived at a bad time," said Joanne, turning to Rosemary. Maybe we should wait until after they've had their dinner."

"Or maybe we should wait a *few more years*. That woman is quite scary; she reminds me of my gran!" A scrawny cat padded by, its tail loosely wrapped in a bandage. "Poor cat," Rosemary remarked. The cat presently sat down and pulled at the bandage with its teeth until the material fell to the ground. The tail underneath looked undamaged, and the cat promptly leapt onto a windowsill and proceeded to wash itself. Rosemary realised that the animal was probably only victim to young Mary's training.

"Take two!" Joanne announced as they disembarked the TP once again. This time it was raining lightly, in a manner that was quite refreshing, very unlike the kind of annoying rain that one got in England. And Joanne had dared to land nearer to the Hall this time, despite Rosemary's reservations.

"It'll be fine!" Joanne said, dismissively, as she locked up once again. Rosemary tapped Joanne's arm in a frenzied manner.

"Look, look, it's her!" she whispered. "She's a few years older, but it's definitely her again."

Both looked on to see a teenage Mary, standing with a hold-all at her feet and her mother's arms wrapped around her. The mother was audibly bawling and neighbours were also present, apparently bidding farewell. The mother pulled away, wiped the tears from her daughter's face and then from her own.

"Now nuh figet tuh sen pan fi mi luv an behave while yuh inna company ah fi wi dear relatives."

"Mi will ma," Mary replied with a sniff.

"What did she tell her?" Joanne whispered to Rosemary.

"Her mum told her to remember to send her love to their relatives and to behave, basically. She must be going to stay with them."

"This must be the first time she left home. She looks so young and everyone's so emotional."

Mother and daughter drew apart and Mary hauled her bag onto her back, looking back only once as she waved off onlookers. Once the farewell party had dispersed, Joanne and Rosemary hurried to her side. Rosemary was eager to talk to her.

"Waa gwaan," she ventured in greeting. She had felt confident saying it in Montego Bay, after all. The girl stopped and looked at her, pulled her load higher up her back and squinted. She was young and cautious of the sudden presence of a stranger; it was only to be expected. Mary smiled and responded, "Irie." Mary told her that everything was all right.

"Where are you going?" she asked, then fumbled over her words, not wanting to sound creepy. "I mean, are you off travelling?"

"Mi gwine England tuh learn bout medicine."

"Fantastic. My friend and I are from England." She gestured to Joanne who beamed her most Joanne smile. Mary could not help but smile back at the island's newcomers.

Mary asked what England was like, but Rosemary didn't know where to start, especially in the 1800s. Should she gush about how friendly and fantastic some people could be or warn her about how narrow minded and nasty they could be, or both? Joanne butted in before she could respond.

"Oh, you will love it. It's a land of opportunity, with … lots of potential. But be on your guard." It was evident from Mary's face that she was struggling with both semantics and dialect, but she smiled all the same. "You're young so be careful, but don't be afraid to live your dream."

"It's not easy being a black woman in a white male world," said Rosemary, suddenly serious. "But I have a feeling that you'll thrive. Besides, you can always come back."

"Mi tink mi undastan," Mary said. Still not feeling that today was the day for adding to their autograph collection, the two girls let the teenager go on her way.

"Criss luck!" Rosemary called after her.

"So, the question now is, do we follow her and meet up with her in England?"

"At the risk of sounding like a stalker whichever direction we choose," said Rosemary, "I would like to meet grown-up Mary in her prime, helping wounded soldiers in the Crimean War."

"In the *war*?" Joanne asked with a gulp. "I know we're extreme autograph hunters, but that doesn't sound very safe."

"I don't plan on landing on the front line Jo, but don't you think it would be cool to see the British Hotel; the hospital which she set up?"

"I don't know, Rosie. I'm not sure my immune system's up to it."

"OK, you're probably right. She'll probably be too busy to chat and sign autographs anyway," Rosemary conceded.

"Rather than venturing out to Crimea, why not wait here for her? It's so beautiful and there's so much history here. According to my clandestine Google search, she was likely here in the 1840s, after she got married."

"OK. It'll be interesting to see how much travel has changed her."

Once again, the girls used the Temporal Perambulator to travel further along Mary Seacole's timeline. Joanne didn't let on, but she could not be a hundred per cent sure that she had inputted the exact time co-ordinates. The TP had felt like it had been pulling to the left, like a poorly aligned motorcar. Her suspicions grew when they landed three metres due south from where they had departed. It was not easy combining Sir Cuthbert's fictional time co-ordinates with places the character hadn't even been to. Triangulating a needle in a haystack, from a fictional universe in an improbable time machine. Rosemary didn't seem to notice that they had disembarked in a different place, however, as she was too busy picking a stone from between her toes.

She grumbled and hurled the stone across the ground. It bounced off a wall. A newly painted wall.

"Is it me, or does Blundell Hall look a bit different to you?" she asked.

"It does seem to have had a bit of a face-lift, now you come to mention it," replied Jo, peering upwards.

"A face-lift? It looks as though it's been completely rebuilt."

The building was indeed recognisable as Blundell Hall, but it was as though a brand-new building had been erected in its stead.

"Dat a bicause ih hav bin rebuilt," piped up the voice of an elderly gentleman. The girls spun around. "Di wul place burned dun, neva yuh aware?"

"We were not aware, no," said Rosemary. "Do the family still live here?" The gentleman took off his tattered hat and looked down at the ground.

"Mrs Grant gaan tuh heaven, much tuh har children's distress. Shi dead nuh lang afta Mary's usband dead."

"Mary's husband died too?" Rosemary felt crestfallen, though she didn't even know the family. "And their children? What became of them?"

"Mary an Edwin's chillun?"

Rosemary nodded, desperate for information. These were her ancestors after all. The man looked up and told her plainly, "Weh yuh bin? Mary n Edwin didn't ave nuh chillun."

15

"But … she must have. I'm a descend … I'm a … "

"Yuh ah what? Reporter?"

"No, no, it doesn't matter."

The man put his hat back on in a dramatic fashion and continued on his way, muttering to himself.

Rosemary shook Joanne by the shoulders as though forcing her to comprehend. "She had no children. So that means I can't be related to her. Mary Seacole is not my family, Joanne!"

"Are you *sure* you have this right?" Joanne peeled her friend's hands off her shoulders and sat her down on the steps of the building. "Are you really going to take the words of a passing old geezer on something so important?"

"I … I don't know. All this time, my mother was so *sure*. Why would she lie? Why? How would you feel if you found out your great-great-great whatever grandmother wasn't who you thought she was?"

"I have no idea who my great-great-great grandmother was, but I see your point."

Rosemary sobbed into her hands, truly exasperated. Joanne put a comforting hand on her back and looked at the building properly for the first time. The wood-panelled structure stood on several feet of brick foundation, with jalousie blinds where one might expect glass windows to be. Through the front door, she could just make out a covered piazza area which was home to rocking chairs and hammocks, primarily all occupied. The occupants didn't look in the best of health and Joanne recognised the person who was tending to them. Joanne felt guilty for having brought her friend to this time and place and not to Crimea where she had wished to go – a time before Edwin, before Mary's mother's death and before there were no children. Joanne puzzled the logistics of this impossible conundrum in her head for a few moments then stood up. As the sun rose to its pinnacle, the heat was relentless and there was no available shade.

"Come one," said Joanne. "Let's go inside."

"I thought you didn't want to be around sick people?"

"I'll keep my distance."

The screen door was unlocked and the girls tentatively let themselves into the Hall. They were hit with a cacophony of smells – flowers in the piazza had evidently been placed in an attempt to mask the odour of mustard emetics, vomit and the familiar acetone scent of death. Undeterred, they ventured in, hopeful that the airy piazza would keep them safe. A woman in her forties, her long dark hair parted in the centre and tied up in a practical fashion, was supporting a frail man as he stepped into the piazza. She helped him to a rocking chair and brought him a bundle of cloths which she tucked in across his legs. Despite the heat of the day, the man appeared to be shivering and gratefully accepted a drink from her. The woman was speaking to him in low, kind tones, empathy spilling out of her every pore. Once she was satisfied that he was comfortable, she offered a young woman a drink also.

"Mi feel sick," the young woman croaked.

"Mi wi fetch unnu medicine soon. Jus wait ah while langa," came the response, gentle but firm.

"Hello," Rosemary braved and the woman turned around, her skirts brushing the floor. "Are you Mary Seacole?"

"Mmm-hmm. A yuh sick?"

"No."

"Den git out eff yuh waan tuh tan well," the woman gestured.

"*What* did she say?" Joanne whispered, unable to fully follow the thick creole.

"I *think* she said that we should get out if we want to stay well," replied Rosemary, a little unsure herself.

"What is wrong with your patients?" asked Joanne.

"Dem mostly hab cholera," she said and put her hands on her hips. Joanne could see the family resemblance with the mother they had seen here before. This *must* be grown-up Mary.

"Then we will be OK," she said, confidently. "It's not contagious."

"Are you *sure*?" Rosemary looked at her, wide-eyed.

"Unless we drink infected water or come into contact with any sewage, we should be fine."

"Do you have a moment?" Rosemary asked, while they still had Mrs. Seacole's attention. She approached the woman and could barely stop the smile from seeping through her lips. "You're a hero. It is an honour to meet you."

"Hab yuh travelled fur jus tuh si mi?" Mary seemed both flattered and confused.

"Yes. I know you're very busy. I have one or two questions. But first, I am sorry to hear about your husband and mother."

The woman simply nodded, her brave expression barely waning.

"I know this is a personal question," she faltered, hoping that her dialect and accent was not too hard for her to understand. "But is it true that you and Edwin did not have children?"

"Duh yuh *si* any chil'ren?" Mary responded, gesturing around her at the lack of any offspring at her feet. Her voice was slightly raised, brow furrowed.

"I ... I'm sorry I was just curious if you have or ever ..."

"Di time hav passed," she said with a shake of her head. Her voice softer, now. "Mi hab nuh regrets. Mi ave fi mi patients."

"Of course. Thank you. Er and the second question is ..." The girls simultaneously held out their autograph books.

After a moment of confusion and a look of realisation followed by a shrug of exasperation, Mary floundered with the ball-point pen and scrawled the form of her name in both books. It looked as though Mary was going to ask them something in return, when she was distracted suddenly by the sound of the young woman throwing up into a bowl. Mary walked calmly to her aid, turning back to say, "Excuse mi."

Rosemary gave a half wave and a nod. "Maybe it's not appropriate to hang around here too long."

"Now that you've got what you came for?" Joanne tutted.

"I didn't come here just for her autograph. I came here for her answer."

Joanne said nothing and creaked open the screen door. They padded back down the warm stone steps and onto the dusty ground. Rosemary looked up at the Hall once more, as though saying goodbye. The tears in her eyes glistened in the sunlight.

"Are you OK?" asked Joanne. Rosemary shrugged.

"I will be. I'm just having an identity crisis at the moment. Why would my mum lie like that, Jo? It makes no sense."

"It's not the most malicious lie in the world. But it is an odd one." Joanne paused. "Do you want to meet Mary again? We can go forwards to the Crimean War this time, or back in time to her wedding or ..."

"There's no point," said Rosemary with a sigh. "We've done what we came to do. Anything else would just be rubbing salt into the wound. It was wonderful to see her in her prime and it makes it all the more real, but I just have so many questions now!" Exasperation was giving way to resentment and rage now.

"So, I suppose the only logical place to go next is twentieth-century England. To ask your mum these questions."

"Not yet," Rosemary protested. "I need to calm down a bit first. I need to sleep on it at least. Anyway, it's your turn to choose."

"If you insist," said Joanne.

"I think the Temporal Perambulator has ideas of its own about where we're going next!" Joanne shrieked and clung onto the interior walls. The machine was doing more than pulling slightly to the left now. In fact, it had hummed out of Kingston before she even had time to input any co-ordinates. Rosemary fell to her knees. She yelped as her flesh hit the hard brushed-metal deck. The cramped interior of the TP made it all the more uncomfortable as she held on to nothing for dear life. Moments later the machine stopped shaking for long enough to allow its occupants to stand up, before one final jolt.

"Hey!" Joanne shouted at it. "Why are you being so violent with us?"

Rosemary, feeling nauseated, opened the door. She looked up to be greeted by someone who looked very familiar. "Gran?"

16

"Who are you calling *Gran?*" asked the woman. Despite her smooth complexion, she had Rosemary's gran's eyes, smile and hair, but her voice ... there was something jarring about that accent. *Is it transatlantic?* It certainly wasn't a Jamaican accent. It was impossible to place.

"Sorry about the rough landing. I don't think the TP is very happy with us." The woman was wearing clothes in a style that Rosemary didn't recognise. She was also wearing the smuggest expression that she had ever seen. Rosemary continued to examine the face before her when another face appeared in the doorway. This one had a cheeky smile and was framed by a plethora of unruly curls.

"Ooh, it worked!" The woman clapped her hands. Her voice was slightly weathered by age. "I told you this would work, Rosie. I *remember* it working when we were ... them!"

"You're ... you're *us?*" Rosemary asked, her words sticking in her gullet like unfamiliar food.

Present-day Joanne stepped out of the TP and placed her hands on her hips. She squared up to her counterpart and narrowed her eyes.

"All right. What's going on? Is this a kidnapping?"

"If I remember correctly, you've just been to see Mary, haven't you?" Joanne's counterpart asked Rosemary, ignoring her other self.

"Yes," said Rosemary, a little frostily.

"I know it's a tough time and it's all a bit raw at the moment," empathised the older Rosemary. "But things will work out. You'll see."

"Please tell us what's happening here," pleaded Rosemary.

"You're back at the Ballington Hotel," she replied, simply. "Only it's the year 2060. Alistair and Jeremy are about to join Joanne and I in there. It's hilarious! It's going to really mess with their heads."

"Well, you're really messing with *my* head," said Joanne. "So, the TP isn't broken. It was *you* all along?"

The mischievous counterparts nodded.

"But why?"

"So that you can stay ahead of the game, of course. You are the *ultimate autograph hunters*. You're – *we're* – the champions of this game."

"Those costumes are looking a bit worse for wear," the older Rosemary noted. Rosemary felt instantly judged. Then wondered how exactly she was *supposed* to feel. She had hidden from herself along her own timeline before when they had teamed up with the boys to defeat the bandits, but to actually have a conversation with an older version of oneself was more intimidating than she had imagined. The person in front of her knew all about her; her history, her thoughts and what was to come next. It was difficult to know how to react or what to say. The other Rosemary spoke again before she had the chance to. "I know it's a bit weird. I remember feeling a bit confused when I was you."

"*Bit weird* is an understatement," Rosemary scoffed.

"But because we remember this happening from your point of view, we need to honour the science and show you what we saw."

"OK. I think ..." said Joanne.

"Fantastic!" Future Joanne clapped her hands gleefully for the second time.

The girls had indeed found themselves in the Ballington Hotel. It had an unnerving, uncanny resemblance to the hotel that they had left behind several decades beforehand. They were in a storage room of sorts, with a few folded chairs and tables propped up against one wall and some nondescript boxes and containers along another. The walls themselves appeared to be comprised of vast screens upon which was a confusing display of what looked like old-fashioned wallpaper. Some of the panels were glitching, as though they had been poorly maintained. The view from the only window was obscured by a blind. Joanne went to prise open the slats of the blind, when it suddenly zoomed up out of existence, exposing an extraordinary vista. She gasped.

"Well, it doesn't look very glamourous in here. But *that view!*" She gaped at the quadrangle outside, flanked by tall, glittering edifices. In the centre of the quad sat a grandiose fountain, spurting water in blues, greens and bronze into a diamond-shaped pool below. "And the buildings are so tall! How many floors are there?" She craned her neck to try and see.

"Several hundred in each block, I expect," said future Joanne.

"And the cars ... where are they? I can't even see roads out there," Rosemary observed. At that moment, a fleet of globular vehicles buzzed past the window, the light reflected from the paintwork almost dazzling them. "And what are those people over there wearing? Are they in cosplay?" Rosemary strained to see a group passing in the distance. They were enveloped in coloured material from neck to toe, with striped sashes about their middles and only their heads and hands were visible. The clothes looked so restrictive that the wearers almost had to hop in order to get anywhere.

"No, that's just modern dress here in 2060. Among the younger people, at least. It's interesting walking around the hotel though. There are still Stormtroopers, Cybermen, Wizards and the like. People have been 3D-printing their costumes for a while by this point. Apart from at the Faerie Gathering. They're still kind of old-school."

The girls looked at each other.

"Don't even think about it, younger-me," older Rosemary warned. "You're here to spy on the boys and us in the Green Room."

"But why?" asked Rosemary. "If I wasn't having an identity crisis before, then I certainly am now!"

"Because you need some light relief on your travels. And maybe a comfortable bed for the night."

"All of that is true," Joanne conceded.

"First thing's, first," said older Joanne. "Take a look!" Joanne tapped one of the working wall panels and then ran her fingers over a keypad which appeared at her fingertips. The keyboard vanished from the screen just as quickly and the scene on the panel turned into one of another room. The image was crystal clear and it was almost as though they could step through. "You can watch proceedings on here," she said, in matter-of-fact tones. We shall only be in the next room."

Rosemary and Joanne looked at each other and shrugged. Rosemary's head was already in turmoil. Another dollop of confusion would either add to the turbulence or cure her. At this point it was fifty/fifty. Rosemary opened her mouth to speak, but her older self put her finger to her lips to shush her and she discovered that it was hard to disobey. She watched as their counterparts left the room and then appeared on the screen in front of them.

"I suppose that's the Green Room," said Joanne as they watched their older selves sit down on a long sofa. They watched with apprehension.

"Come in, come in," older Rosemary said, and they heard a door close.

"I'm glad that you came!" said older Joanne.

"We didn't have much choice, did we?" It was Alistair. It was strange to see the boys again. Joanne found herself waving and then realised that they could see her no more than Mathias Price could when the camera was on him.

"We were on our way to *finally* get Jesus's autograph when we find ourselves flung into the future where the infuriating faeries have become celebrities – what's happening?" Jeremy was obviously as annoyed and confused as she was.

"Calm down and we shall explain all," said future Rosemary. There was some shuffling around while the scruffy, well-travelled boys sat down.

"I'm really worried that you've messed up the future – you shouldn't *be* here. And you shouldn't be being so ridiculously conspicuous," said Jeremy. "Headlining a convention, no less!" He folded his arms in defiance.

"*Headlining a convention?*" present-day Joanne mouthed, wide-eyed.

"We are headlining the convention because in 2060 we're successful script writers," said older Rosemary.

"Let me guess – for a show about faeries?" Alistair snorted.

"No, actually. It's a show about ... time travel."

"We've been favouring science fiction over fantasy of late, for reasons which I am sure are evident. And we had plenty of experience, so we thought that we would combine our knowledge and collaborate our ideas," added much older Joanne. "We befriended the right contacts, worked hard on our writing skills and the rest is history ... or future, depending on your point of view."

"No, no, no, no. That's so unfair!" said Jeremy. "If it wasn't for us, you wouldn't even have been able to –"

"Let me get this straight," Alistair interrupted. "You wrote a story for a television programme, based on travelling in a time machine which was from another television programme ..."

"Did I say that?" asked older Joanne, rather crossly. "Look at the leaflet more closely."

"Not those freaky things again," said Jeremy. The girls heard a tune emitting from the pile of leaflets on the table, which crescendoed when Alistair opened one. This was all too much. Both Rosemary and Joanne struggled to process what was unfolding in front of them. But there were more surprises to come.

"Ah, here we are!" There was the sound of a door opening and closing and two elderly gentlemen appeared on the wall-panel screen. They were wearing faded jeans, hooded sweaters and flat plimsolls, but were unquestionably older versions of the boys.

"I need to sit down!" gasped Joanne. "This is all a bit too much. I know we've seen different versions of ourselves, but I'm not sure I want to see too much of the future."

"I trust us to know what we're doing," said Rosemary, after a pause. Nevertheless, she slid down onto the floor next to Joanne before her legs gave way. They continued to watch.

"Thanks for coming, your timing is perfect as ever," said Joanne, standing up and giving both men a hug. "Guys, I'd like you to meet young Jeremy Cope and Alistair Barker."

"Nice to meet you, Alistair," said the taller of the gentlemen. Alistair smiled and shook the man's hand. Older Alistair shook Jeremy's hand.

"Nice to greet you, Jezebel. Blimey jimey, you've always been ugly, haven't you?"

"You're ... you're us?" Their older selves had been right, thought Rosemary. This *was* hilarious.

"But you two – you two don't look much older than when we last saw you. That doesn't make sense," Jeremy pointed at the older women. "Are you the same age as our older selves or have you had some crazy futuristic work done? Which version *are* you?"

"That would be telling, wouldn't it?" Older Rosemary tapped her nose.

"You're not going to tell us? You bring us all the way here only to douse us in *more* mystery?"

"Oh, they'll never stop being infuriating," chuckled the older Jeremy. "It's just something you'll have to get used to. Isn't that right, Mrs Cope?" He shuffled along his seat a little closer to Rosemary and planted a kiss on her cheek.

"Mrs Cope? You mean …"

"Mrs Rosemary Cope and Mrs Joanne Barker at your service," the older women said in unison.

"I remember how I felt when we were in your shoes. Literally," said older Alistair, looking down at the cosplayer's polisher's feet. "I can appreciate how much of a shock this must be to you and also how amazing you're feeling. To this day I still don't understand why the girls insisted on proposing in this way."

"Proposing?" Rosemary and Joanne stared at each other. Rosemary felt faint and was glad that she was already seated. Was any of this real? Perhaps they were acting. Why would their future selves show them this?

"Well what else would you call it? You showed our younger selves that in the future they'd be married to you, thus putting the suggestion in our heads. And I even remember me saying this and thinking, why don't I just stop here, so I will," older Alistair added.

"Much appreciated," said the younger Alistair. "I don't think my brain can cope with much more."

"Likewise," murmured Joanne and Jeremy in unison.

"So why did you bring us here?"

"To show you these." The older versions of the boys revealed two very full autograph books.

"You filled it?"

"You've barely begun your adventures, young me."

"So, Jesus's *isn't* the final autograph we get?" asked Jeremy, his eyes never leaving the battered book in the aged hands of his future self. "We *do* get his autograph, don't we?"

"It wouldn't be much fun if I told you, would it?" replied the older Jeremy.

"Hmm. *Spoilers*. You've become as cryptic as them!"

"We learned from the best," Alistair said with a wink.

"So, what happens now?"

"Now you continue your adventures – we simply wanted to give you some encouragement," said Rosemary.

"You've certainly given us fuel to fry our brains," said Alistair. "But hang on – I have so many questions – how come the time machine is real? It's just from a television show. How does it work?"

"Oh we haven't finished our adventures yet," said Joanne. "We're still to find that out ourselves."

"I don't know who's more annoying – the boys, older them or older us," hissed Joanne.

"I think two Alistairs in one room is the most annoying combination. Or three. Or four."

"I think one would be just enough!" said Joanne, before she could stop herself.

"You *do* like him, don't you?" Rosemary gasped, beaming. Joanne looked coy for probably the first time in her life. Rosemary, who could never put up with Alistair's mood swings and unpredictability, was glad that Joanne liked him. It meant that Rosemary was free to concentrate on Jeremy; reliable, witty – if a little neurotic – Jeremy. When Rosemary was focused again, she realised that the boys' older selves were signing *their own signatures* in their younger selves' autograph books. She laughed so loudly at this absurdity that everyone on the screen looked towards the door. Or did she just imagine it? She clamped a hand over her mouth, just in case.

The rest of the scene unfolded in a bit of a blur and raised more questions than it answered. But the part that stuck most in Rosemary's mind was the proposal. How was it a proposal and when and how would any of the party acknowledge it? Were they really going to be guests at a future convention? And how had their older selves aged much better than the men had? Was any of this real or had their future selves become bigger tricksters with age? By the look on Joanne's face, she was just as confused. She wasn't sure that she wanted to hang around and wait for their older selves to come back from the Green Room.

"Come on, Jo," she said. "I think it's time I met my mother."

"What about that offer of a bed for the night?" Joanne protested.

"On a con weekend? Jo, there aren't going to be any rooms free tonight."

"You make a very good point. Let's go."

17

"My brain feels like its neurons are stuck in a blender," said Joanne as the TP disappeared from the hotel. "I'm not sure if that little kidnapping escapade has helped us or will ultimately send us completely mad!"

"You saw our future selves. I think we know the answer to that one!" said Rosemary. "Seriously though, I suddenly feel overwhelmed by the pressure to achieve all of those things!"

"But it must be doable."

"If we are telling the truth, then I suppose so."

"Why would we lie to ourselves?"

"Maybe all that botox went to our heads!" gasped Rosemary.

"The TP seems to be working properly now. It's a much smoother ride."

"I noticed that too," said Rosemary. "What year are you taking us to, anyway?"

"I've been thinking about that. Hmm ... *what would Sir Cuthbert do?*" Joanne mused.

"What do you mean?"

"I mean, would Sir Cuthbert cross his own childhood timeline, or would that be breaking too many of the rules? Do you think he would be more likely to visit his mother before he was born?"

"*What would Sir Cuthbert do*, eh?" repeated Rosemary. "Now there's an idea for your next tattoo!"

"I don't think Jeremy would be very amused by that."

"Oh, I don't know," said Rosemary with a shrug.

"I think it would be too much of a risk to meet your own mother *before* she had you. Any little thing you might say might sway her into going down a different path like not meeting your father, choosing not to have kids or not completing some random routine that would lead to your eventual birth. Besides, she wouldn't have many answers for you at that stage."

"You could be right. Hey, what if us meeting Mary Seacole as a child led to her somehow not having children and therefore not being my grandmother?"

"Then you wouldn't be standing here talking to me now. Your brain really is fried, isn't it?"

"Just fetch the ketchup and white bread," said Rosemary with a sigh. "This whole grandfather paradox is more complicated than I thought."

"OK, let's just go. Let's go and meet your mum before she got ill," said Joanne in a way that made the decision seem final.

"OK," said Rosemary quietly, a lump forming in her throat.

Joanne managed to programme the TP using information from Rosemary and the aid of the trusty co-ordinates book. The two friends successfully landed in 1994.

"Where are we?" Rosemary asked as a fairy light smacked her in the face, followed by a tree branch. "Narnia?"

"In your childhood local park," said Joanne, as though it was obvious.

"In the middle of a Christmas tree?"

"I thought it would be nice to arrive in December. Childhood Christmases are the most magical ones, after all."

"But, in the middle of a Christmas tree?" Rosemary repeated.

"Well, that element wasn't exactly planned," Joanne conceded as she held back a large branch so her friend could squeeze through. It was Rosemary's turn to look after the Golden Knob and she struggled to lock it with a face full of twigs and a dozen fairy lights dazzling her. They battled their way through into a twilit park. A few steps took them across the square of grass, in which the tree was the centre. They made their way down a deserted footpath and headed towards a gate.

"I used to love playing here when I was little," remembered Rosemary. "We used to pretend that the benches were boats, and the stream was a great river. It always looked so beautiful at Christmas and if it snowed, we would take our sledges up to that hill over there. It doesn't even look like a hill now. It's barely even a slope. But to us, it was a *mountain*."

"*Us?*"

"The neighbours' kids and me. And my cousins too. Although when my big cousin Michael came over we could go to the big park with the play area, but that was a bit of a walk and across a busy road. My parents preferred us to play here though when Michael wasn't here, as they could see the whole area from the upstairs window. That was our house, look." Rosemary pointed to one of the townhouses which bordered the square. "It's owned by a new family now. It's weird to see it like this again with the old front door and that tatty old snowman on the porch roof. It had seen better days even then!"

"The house is impressive though," said Joanne. "I bet it's worth a bit now, too."

"It had too many stairs," groaned Rosemary. "My mum really struggled to get up the two flights in the end and had to have her bedroom moved to the ground floor."

"Ah that's tough," said Joanne. "Pancreatic cancer, wasn't it?"

"Yes."

"That one's an aggressive bugger. I'm so sorry."

Rosemary nodded, wiping away a tear. "It was a long time ago. It would be so strange to see her again." She found her sense of humour again; "We can't exactly knock on her door like she's William Shakespeare."

"What was her name again? I'm terrible remembering the names of my mates' parents. You know how it is!"

"Emma."

Joanne smiled and nodded.

"Hey, who's that kid?" Joanne nudged her as they reached the gate.

"It's Michael!" Rosemary cried. "Aw he was so adorable at that age. I always looked up to him and thought of him as so much older. But he must be about thirteen. I remember that turquoise shell suit. He was rarely in anything else!"

"Even by 1994? I thought it was an eighties thing."

"Michael made up his own rules."

"Fair play. What's he doing? He can't be calling this late, surely."

"It seems late," agreed Rosemary. "But it's winter. It could be five o'clock for all we know."

"As accurate as the TP is, it could do with a compatible clock on the wall!"

The two of them remained by the gate, their eyes on Rosemary's childhood home. The door opened and Michael was talking to someone. Her mother? Her heart began to pound and the lump in her throat grew bigger. She was wearing a woolly jumper and a knee-length skirt and tights. A small child appeared between her knees.

"That's me! I used to hide behind my mum's legs all the time, I was so shy. Even if it was just my cousin. It would take me so long to come out of my shell, even with familiar people around."

"What does Michael want?" asked Joanne, resting a hand on the gate.

"I can't remember this exact day!" Rosemary laughed. "But, knowing Michael, he was probably on his way to the local Spar and asking my mum if she wanted anything."

"What a sweetie."

"He really was. I should get in touch with him again, it's been a while. Hey – I've just had an idea. How's your singing voice?"

Rosemary knocked on the door of her childhood home. Nostalgia washed over her in a warm, but salty, wave as she gazed at the homemade wreath that hung inches from her nose. She could smell the clementine scent that her mum used so liberally around the home at this time of year. Memories overflowed in her mind – bittersweet – special Christmases enjoyed with both her parents and evenings by the fireside. But there was also the painful loss of her mother – that aching hollowness that would never completely fade.

This is a stupid idea, she thought. But just then the door swung open. It was her mother again, sans child at her knees. Her mother's eyes were warm but tired, and her smile was weary but welcoming.

"God rest ye merry gentlemen, may nothing you dismay," began the girls. "Remember Christ your saviour was born on Christmas day …" The woman bobbed in time to the tune and her smile grew, as though she wanted them to continue. Rosemary looked at Joanne then back at her mother, fighting back tears and focusing on the song. "Er …To save us all from Satan's power when we were gone astray, glad tidings of comfort and joy, comfort and joy, glad tidings of comfort and joy."

At a loss as to how the next verse went, Rosemary faltered and then Joanne stopped awkwardly, mid-sentence. Rosemary's mother clapped and busied herself with a handbag which hung on a coat hook in the long hallway. She offered two one-pound coins, accompanied by a wide smile. Unthinkingly, Rosemary accepted them and thanked her, her eyes fixed on her mother.

"Er ..." she faltered again. "Do you, er ..."

Joanne nudged her.

"Can I er ..."

"Muuuuum!" Rosemary heard her younger self call from another room. "Hurry uuuuup!"

"That's my little Rosie. I had better go and see what she wants. Beautiful singing, girls. Thank you." She looked at Joanne and then back at Rosemary. "You remind me of someone. Hang on ... are you ... are you *Lucy's* girl?" Lucy was Rosemary's aunt, Emma's estranged sister who had lived in fifteen countries throughout her life, but never England. "Forgive me, but there's something familiar about your eyes and your stance. I don't know why I didn't spot you straight away."

"Yes, Emma, this is – " started Joanne, her mouth moving faster that her brain.

"– Caroline," finished Rosemary, whose brain had also not properly engaged with reason.

"Of course it is!" Emma enthused. "Then what are you doing standing on my doorstep in the cold, singing to me before even saying hello? And why didn't my sister call ahead?"

Rosemary held out her arms and grinned awkwardly. "Er ... surprise!"

18

"Come in, come in ... where are your bags? Aren't you stopping?" Rosemary remembered how accommodating her mother could be – and trusting too. They had literally just stepped off the street in the busiest city in the country, with no proof of who they were. Before they could respond, Emma asked, "And why are you treading the streets dressed like that, in mid-winter? You'll catch a death."

"Oh, this is warm to me," lied Rosemary. "I've been living in er ... Norway for the last three years with Mum, so an English winter seems practically tropical."

"Of course," said Emma, ushering them into the lounge and immediately turning up the fire to three bars.

"Besides, we thought it would be fun to dress as faeries for little Rosie's sake!" said Joanne and flashed a smile at the small child by the Christmas tree.

"Muuum!" young Rosemary whined. "When's Dad home?"

"In a little while, Rosie. Now why don't you come and meet your cousin Caroline and her friend ..."

"Joanne," replied Joanne, opting to use her own name in a bid to keep things simple.

"Have you flown in from Norway too? You don't sound Norwegian, nor local to be honest. You and Caroline have probably travelled more than Mary Seacole, haven't you? I expect you've picked up all kinds of accents and dialects from all over with your mum living in ... how is your mum?"

Rosemary looked at her friend.

"She's doing OK thanks. She er … she says hello and sends her love."

Joanne realised where Rosemary had got some of her nervousness from, and also some of her enthusiasm. Emma seemed nothing if not eager to see them. But Joanne was worried. The longer they spent here, the more dangerous things could become. Rosemary had crossed her own timeline. Although young Rosemary was here, one false move could change anything. *Or was that what Rosemary was trying to do? Was Rosemary trying to save her mother?*

"Would you girls like a mug of mulled cider?" Emma asked, plumping up some cushions and inviting the girls to sit down. They accepted the offer and made themselves comfortable. Joanne stretched out her feet in front of her and took advantage of the heat of the fire. "Give me a minute or two while I heat it up," Emma called from the kitchen.

"What if young you comes over to talk to us?" Joanne whispered.

"She won't. She's too shy," Rosemary reassured her. She eyed little Rosie playing beneath the tree, surrounded by fairy lights and playing with her dolls. Despite her apparent attention on the toys, Rosemary noticed her curious glances and met them with a smile.

"What's going on here, Rosemary?" Joanne asked her plainly.

"What do you mean?"

"What's your plan?"

"Plan?"

"Don't play dumb. What are you trying to do here?"

"What do you mean?"

"Are you going to warn your mum about the cancer? You're going to try and save her, aren't you?" She made it sound like an accusation.

"Is that what you think? Oh, Jo, if only I could! But by this point, the disease already has hold of her. I can see through that weak smile and behind those sparkling eyes. She's in pain. That smile was wider and those eyes shone brighter the Christmas before."

"Very poetic," said Joanne. "But seriously, you don't plan on going back further and trying to save her, do you? And to save yourself from all the grief in the process?"

"I haven't got the power to do that, Jo. It's a deadly disease with a five per cent survival rate – warning or no warning. And even if I *could* save her, then I wouldn't grow up to be me, I wouldn't find solace in fantasy and science fiction and I wouldn't be going to conventions, therefore …"

"Therefore, you wouldn't have found the time machine …" finished Joanne. "That damn grandfather paradox is back again."

"Precisely." Rosemary turned to her younger self. "Hey, Rosie, are those Flower Fairies?" Rosemary remembered the Heliotrope and Sweet Pea dolls in her hands. She probably still had them somewhere. Little Rosemary nodded.

"Fairies are the best!" she proclaimed, triumphantly, before adding, "I like your costumes."

"Thank you," said Rosemary, aware that they probably smelled pretty awful by this point; they certainly weren't worthy attire for visiting long lost relatives.

"Here you are girls, nice and hot," announced Emma as she placed the mugs on the largest table from a nest in the corner. "Just leave them to cool a while." She dragged out a smaller table from the nest and placed her own mug on it.

"I heard you talking to Caroline and Joanne, Rosie, that's nice," said Emma, filled with praise for her shy daughter. Young Rosemary giggled and padded across the room to find a book to hide behind.

Typical me, thought Rosemary.

"You must have been Rosie's age when I last saw you. Although I've seen pictures," said Emma. "Your mum and dad used to send them over and then I suppose we just lost touch."

"That's a shame," said Joanne. *If it had been a couple of decades later the sisters would have had the advantage of the internet to keep in touch*, she thought.

"Indeed," said Emma.

"I have a question, Aunt Emma," said Rosemary and passed a mug to Joanne. She took the other for herself and blew on the contents. Her olfactory system was flooded with apple, cinnamon, cloves and nutmeg. She breathed it in, letting the warmth travel through her lungs.

"Go on," said Emma, warming her clasped hands over her own mug.

"I remember when we lived in London that Gran used to talk about Mary Seacole. Was she … was she related to us?"

"Great-great grandma Mary!" piped up young Rosie, before ducking behind her book again. Emma glanced at her young daughter then back at her older version.

"My, you've got a good memory. What makes you ask that?"

"She used to say it was true. And Mum talks about her a lot too."

"She does?"

"Muuuum!" Rosie interjected. "Can I go and look through your telescope and look for Father Christmas and his reindeer pleeeeeease?"

"Don't interrupt, Rosemary! And no, it's not Christmas Eve yet. You're going to bed as soon as your dad gets in anyway."

"But Muuuuum!"

"Sssh!" Emma admonished.

"I didn't realise I was such a whiny child," Rosemary whispered to Joanne.

"Sorry about that," said Emma.

"That's how kids are," said Joanne with a shrug and sipped her cider. "She's a cutie."

"Thank you sweetie. Anyway Caroline, it's funny you should say that because Mum still talks about our ancestor Mary and I worship the woman, but I didn't think your mum was particularly a fan."

"I er ..."

"But then, she always was a contrary child. What is there *not* to love about Mary Seacole – any more than there is about Florence Nightingale?"

"So, she *is* our ancestor?"

"Not in the traditional sense," said Emma and took another sip. "More someone to look up to. She's half Jamaican, half British like your gran. She is one of the most influential black women in history. She did so much and yet most people of our generation don't seem to talk about her, so your gran and I have always tried to keep her alive in our hearts. It seems daft now I come to say it out loud, but that's the way it is. The idea of her brings us some comfort I suppose. It's still not easy being a black family in a white country, but I'm sure in the next decade or so, things will get easier for us."

Rosemary looked away and bit her tongue in order to stop herself from spilling a few facts from the future. She forced herself to catch her gaze.

"Yes, maybe attitudes will get better."

"Of course they will!"

"Mary Seacole didn't actually have any children ... that's why I was confused."

"You like to spend your time in the library reading the Britannica, do you?" Emma asked with a laugh.

"Something like that, yes."

"Is that what you wanted to ask me? You came a long way."

Rosemary nodded. "Yes, we did come a long way. And that has been on my mind, yes, but that wasn't the only reason. I miss you … Aunty Emma." She blinked away a tear.

"Bless you," said Emma and put down her mug, lunged forwards and drew her in for an embrace. Rosemary was taken aback by the sudden affection from her mum; her mum who had not embraced her in so long. Joanne took the steaming mug from her friend's hand before it spilled onto the floor and Rosemary hugged her mother tighter than she had wanted to for years; more than twenty years of hugs emerged as one.

"Oh!" Emma exclaimed and finally pulled away. "That was a lovely hug!"

"Sorry," said Rosemary.

"Don't apologise."

Rosemary suddenly wondered if her younger self had heard any of their conversation and realised the possible repercussions of her learning the information about her ancestor – or non-ancestor – at this stage in her life. For if she already knew the truth then there would be no need for her to find out, in the future. But young Rosie was fast asleep behind her book, as Emma had just found out.

"Ah, I had better go and take little 'un up to bed. I'll be back in a minute."

"No problem," Rosemary called after her.

"Well that went as well as it could have … as long as you're OK about the whole Mary Seacole thing."

"Yeah, I'm OK about all that. It was something and nothing really."

"Right, so are you ready to go soon?" Joanne asked, downing the last of her drink.

"Go? But we've only just got here. I've waited years to see my mum again. I'm not going anywhere."

* * *

Emma had gone upstairs carrying an infant and had reappeared with her arms full of photo albums.

"Would you like to look through some of these with me?"

"Let the nostalgia commence!" Rosemary exclaimed and put down her mug. She caught Joanne's eye. She did not look happy. *Why was she in such a rush to leave? What was the harm?*

A knock at the door drew Emma away from them once more.

Joanne glanced at the daunting pile of photo albums. Rosemary turned to her.

"Oh come on, Jo. I know this isn't going to be very interesting for you, but please try to understand."

"I'm worried you're going to mess up or say the wrong thing. We are on dodgy ground," hissed Joanne.

"Oh so it's OK for your future self to hurl us through time to show us some crazy stuff or for you to dance with biblical characters, but when I want to spent a bit of time with my *deceased mother*, it's wrong?"

"And now you're getting upset. I'm not sure this is a good idea."

"No, Joanne, *you're* making me upset. I know you want to go and collect autographs – go for it. Here's the Golden Knob. But this is more important to me, than that." Rosemary took out the Golden Knob and handed it to Joanne.

"I *know* it's important. But you have done what you came to do. And I just think it's best we leave now before things get too complicated!"

"And I think it's best that I stay with my mum." She felt rage building up in her belly, fuelled by the cider and her grief.

"Well then I should stay with you and make sure you're OK."

"Whatever," said Rosemary, dismissively.

Emma returned with a carrier bag. "It was only Michael. I told him you were here, but he had to get back to his mum."

"What did he fetch for you?" asked Rosemary, resisting the urge to call her Mum.

"Just some milk and a few festive treats," she said and placed a box of mince pies on one of the tables. "Help yourself."

Rosemary didn't need asking twice and opened the box while Emma took the other groceries into the kitchen. She was beginning to feel at home in more ways than one. She offered one to Joanne who shook her head. Rosemary shrugged and used the tin foil the mince pie came in as a makeshift plate to catch the crumbs.

"OK – one hour. Then we need to go," said Joanne in serious tones.

Rosemary was too engrossed in her snack to respond.

Joanne absent-mindedly picked up one of the photo albums and started to flick through. It was emblazoned with a garish orange and brown pattern and the plastic wrapping was crinkly and worn from use. "You won't really want to touch these with your sticky mince pie fingers," she told Rosemary. Rosemary shrugged and Emma rejoined them, nestling between them on the sofa.

"I see you've chosen 1974. That must have been the last time I saw you and your brother – "

"– And aunt ... er ... my mum," Rosemary stumbled.

"Geezam! That is a long time ago. I really must make the effort and get in touch. Especially now ..."

"Especially now. Since... Caroline, I er... I did try and get in touch. I'm ill, sweetie. And the prognosis isn't good.

Rosemary didn't know how to react to hearing the news a second time. It certainly wasn't any easier. She wasn't sure if it was mince pie or sadness that was clogging her throat. She managed a, "I'm sorry" which was muffled by a hug.

"It's been tough, you know," Emma said, when they finally parted.

Mum must have put on a brave face and tried to hide her vulnerability for my sake, Rosemary realised. *It wasn't until today that I have been able to find out how she had been really feeling. Mum didn't really know her niece, but perhaps the unconscious familiarity of older me is encouraging her to open up. I hope so. But how far do I push?*

"You know, in some ways it's as though the last twenty years have passed in a few minutes!" Emma said, pulling back and looking at Rosemary with watery eyes. Rosemary nodded through her own tears, "I know exactly what you mean."

"Look, there's your mum and dad. Don't they look fabulous in their bell-bottom trousers?" Emma commented, flicking through the album. It was interesting looking at these photographs again, but Rosemary was just cherishing the time she was spending with her mum. Eating mince pies by the fireside and just enjoying her company was priceless. Joanne, however, was becoming restless.

We really need to go, thought Joanne. *This is getting ridiculous. The longer we stay, the higher the risk we're taking. I have a really bad feeling about this.*

The photo album "to read" pile was now shorter than the "read" pile and Emma made the decision that they have a break from reminiscing. She stood up and asked,

"Would either of you like another cider, during this er … intermission?" Emma was laughing, but Joanne could see that she was struggling with fatigue. Why couldn't Rosemary see it too? Was she really so selfish? "Or a hot cup of Jamaican cocoa?"

"Ooh yes please M … . That sounds delicious."

"And you, Joanne?"

"No thank you, Emma. In fact, I need to get going."

"What?" asked Rosemary and Emma in unison.

"I thought you were both staying. There's plenty of room," Emma told her.

"That's really kind of you, but I have family in the area I'd like to visit myself, so I'll see myself out."

"You'll be back in the morning?" asked Emma, a little taken aback.

"Sure," said Joanne, not wishing to sound impolite.

"Well, you're welcome anytime."

Joanne nodded and headed towards the door.

"I'll see you out!" called Rosemary and followed her onto the porch and half closed the door behind her. "What are you doing?" she hissed.

"Come on Rosemary."

"What?" Rosemary could not believe what her friend was suggesting. "We can't leave now!"

"Of course we can! You've spent some quality time with your mother haven't you? There's no harm done if we just slope off."

"No harm done?"

"Apart from the harm you've already done. Because of you, she's going to get in touch with her sister after all these years and the *real* Caroline will no doubt be visiting and she'll realise that you weren't her and there will be a ripple effect just from that one decision. I ... we just can't risk making it worse!"

"But she won't see her again. I don't remember it happening. Mum dies in a few months." Rosemary couldn't hold back any more. She blurted out, *"The next time Lucy visits is at Mum's funeral!"*

"But you don't know that!" Joanne cried, exasperated. "I'm sorry. I just can't wreck the timeline with you, just because you want a cocoa with your mum!"

"That's cold, Joanne," said Rosemary through tears. She grabbed her shoulders. "Really cold."

Joanne pulled away and made her way back towards to main road. "See you around."

Rosemary stood there, gaping, stranded.

19

Well, maybe I'll just stay here forever, thought Rosemary, rage mounting inside her. She stepped back inside the solace of the house and slammed the door behind her. Feeling guilty she called out, "Sorry! The wind blew the door shut."

"That's OK," her mum called back. Her mum. *Her mum!* This was real and it was not fair for Joanne to want to take this away from her. "Your cocoa is ready."

I can't believe how utterly selfish she's being, thought Joanne, walking quickly to burn off the adrenaline which was pumping around her system. *Sure, there are times and places I want to go back to too, but I haven't done that. She can't see past her own grief. Well, if she wants to sit there playing happy families then she's delusional. She'll slip up at some point and it'll all go wrong.*

Joanne threw open the park gate, strode along the moonlit path, stomped across the dewy grass and fought her way through the fir tree to the Temporal Perambulator. Muttering to herself, she let herself in. The small interior of the time machine felt empty and lonely. She opened the door again, changing her mind. *I can't leave her here.* But then she closed it again. *But she made her decision. She chose her dead mother over me. She's finally lost it. I can't even look at her at the moment. But I don't want to be alone either.*

Joanne thought for a moment, consulted the book of co-ordinates and let her fingers cavort across the controls. The time machine faded and surfaced moments later at midnight in 2022 in an exhibition hall at a hotel in Los Angeles. Joanne confidently stepped out and locked the door behind her. She noted the familiar police-box shape, a prop from another well-known television science fiction series, next to where she had landed. She also noticed a DeLorean and a rack of character costumes.

Hidden in plain sight, she said to herself and made for the exit. In contrast to the dim, empty exhibition hall, the hotel hallways were buzzing with life. Surrounded by colourful costumes, happy chatter and the enthusiasm of American sci-fi fans, she no longer felt alone. The lobby seemed to be the social hub of the night, so Joanne found herself a seat and observed the room.

"Do you want to come over and join us?" asked a girl wearing a red wig and a costume which Joanne assumed was attributed to an anime character. She was expertly shuffling a deck of cards and cocked her head at the table behind her. There was another girl dressed like an anime character also, identical twin boys in civilian dress and a young man dressed as the Fourth Doctor. Joanne shrugged and said, "Why not?"

Rosemary snuggled down under crisp sheets and a comfortingly heavy duvet. She lay, foetal-like, and cherished the moment as the layers above her slowly warmed her. Part of her wished that her mum would come in and bid her goodnight as she had done all those years ago. She knew she was too old for a story to be read to her, but longed to again experience the safety and reassurance that such a simple act offered. She could hear her younger self call out in the next room and then heard Emma go in to tend to her. She felt an odd pang of jealousy.

As she drifted off, Rosemary tried to remember whether she had remembered her cousin Caroline visiting her and talking to her about Flower Fairies. Or had she altered the past? Would new memories make themselves known? she wondered.

"Rosemary, come on!" Rosemary woke up to find herself on the front porch of her childhood home. *How did I get here?* Joanne was standing over her with her arms folded and a scowl on her face. She was not wearing her faerie costume, but a dragon outfit with mirrored panels for scales.

"Joanne, what are you wearing?" Rosemary asked as a hundred distorted faces gleamed back at her through the shiny scales.

"Come on. It's ruined. It's all ruined!"

"What's ruined?" Rosemary asked, peeling off a sheet that was wrapped around her, although under the sheet was another sheet and another and then layers of leaves. The leaves twisted into the branches of a fir tree, but they were turning brown and crispy before her eyes with a sickening scream. She tried to stand up, but found that her feet were bound together by a string of fairy lights. The lights were broken, but somehow still lit, and shattered glass dug into her toes. The wire was digging into her ankles. She looked up at Joanne and held out her hand for help. Joanne only continued to scowl and then opened her mouth impossibly wide. A jet of fire roared from her mouth and Rosemary winced. She screamed.

"Are you all right?" It was Emma.

Rosemary opened her eyes to find her mum standing by the door, holding a worried looking toddler – Rosemary. Rosemary nodded, still catching her breath. "I … I'm … it was just a nightmare."

"I get bad dreams too!" said young Rosemary.

"You both must be vivid dreamers," said Emma. "I heard you shouting from the next room. I'll go and put the kettle on."

Rosemary mouthed a thank you and plopped back down onto the pillow.

Maybe my subconscious is telling me that I have ruined everything, she thought.

Joanne had enjoyed some time-out playing a simple card game with random strangers at a sci-fi convention in a city on the other side of the world. She had felt anonymous and accepted, without Rosemary or anyone else judging her or making her do anything; the pressure was off. Except that the card game hadn't been as simple as she had thought, with the instructions taking over half an hour to explain to the group and the game itself taking almost two hours to complete. But it had been fun and she had enjoyed the deck-building experience. She returned her cards to the pack and enthused about the game.

"Did you really fly out here on your own?" one of the twins asked her, whose name was Jason. The cards had been put away and the group were socialising among themselves.

"Yeah, I wanted to go on a trip by myself for a change," Joanne told him. It was the truth. More or less.

"Good for you," he said. "You're real pretty, you know."

"Thanks," she said, but didn't return the complement. "But I'm er … I'm kind of married. *Will* be married."

"Really? Pity." Jason ran a hand through long blonde locks and looked crestfallen. He was attractive, but Joanne had no desire to complicate matters at this juncture. "So where is your husband-, or wife-, to-be then?"

"*– or wife?*" Joanne asked, taken aback.

"Yeah. Wasn't same-sex marriage finally legalised in your country in 2013?"

"I er … yeah, I suppose it was," said Joanne, clueless about anything that had happened between 2012 and 2022.

"Sorry, I didn't mean to pry," he said. "I was just making conversation I guess."

"Not at all, it's fine. I've er … I've had a long day and it's quite a complicated situation to be honest, so …"

"So, you'd rather talk about *Sir Cuthbert's Remarkable Adventures Through Time*?" he offered with a cheeky smile, eyeing her tattoo as she turned her head.

"I'm even a little behind on that," she admitted. "Is there a Faerie Gathering here?"

"Like at the UK ZealCon?" he asked, knowledgeably. Joanne nodded. "No, but there ain't nothing stopping you from starting one, I guess."

"No, no, I was just curious. Let's keep it simple. Are you a fan of Star Wars?"

"The old ones, the new ones or the spin-offs?"

"Just how many are there?" Joanne gasped.

Rosemary chewed through marmalade on toast, but she wasn't really tasting it. She felt a sense of abandonment. Firstly, by her mum, who was about to do so again in a few months' time, and secondly by Joanne. Had she really left her in 1994? *I do want to stay here with her, but how could she have just ditched me?*

"Good morning, Caroline," said her father joining them at the breakfast table. "Emma said you were staying with us."

Rosemary looked up at the very familiar face. How young he looked. There was no hint of grey in his blonde locks and the skin around his blue eyes was smooth. Rosemary was smiling genuinely as he spread marmite thickly onto his own toast.

"Morning," she replied. The last time she had seen him was the day before she left for Zealcon. It seemed so long ago now.

"Are you staying with us for Christmas?" he asked her. "You're welcome to. Your mother too."

"Of course," agreed Emma, pouring herself a cup of tea.

"That's really kind of you, but no. I know Emma is ill and I don't want to impose. Besides, you should concentrate on Rosemary." Rosemary realised she had no idea what the date was until her younger self bounded into the kitchen holding a small piece of chocolate. She called out at a hundred miles an hour "Daddy-Mummy, look-what-I-got in my Advent calendar-today it's a choclit Christmas stocking. Only-seven-more-days to gooooo!"

"That's great Rosemary, now sit down and have your toast."

As predicted, young Rosemary chose marmalade for her topping also and Emma helped her spread it and to cut it into triangles. Her younger self barely acknowledged her presence, but Rosemary knew it was down to shyness rather than rudeness and she took no offence. If anything, Rosemary was jealous of her younger self and the attention she was receiving from her parents. But then she also felt sorry for her. Here was young Rosie in her happy bubble of ignorant bliss, about to have her bubble implode. Then the huge, gaping loss would envelop her and never really leave her.

Only seven more days to go. Rosemary knew she would have to leave before Christmas. She didn't remember her cousin Caroline being there at Christmas. Michael, maybe. But not Caroline. And perhaps Joanne was right. Perhaps it was too big a risk to take. But abandoning her here was not going to help the situation and Joanne should know that.

Joanne opened her eyes and saw that a queue of people was snaking past the rectangular lobby sofa upon which she had fallen asleep. They were clutching autograph books and photos ready to be signed by someone.

"Don't think you can push in the queue from there," snapped a green-haired girl as Joanne sat up and stretched.

"I wasn't planning to," said Joanne with a yawn. "Don't panic. Who are you all queuing for, anyway?"

"Lucinda Humphries from *Sir Cuthbert's Remarkable Adventures Through Time*. Nice tattoo by the way. I like the older series too."

"Er, thanks," said Joanne. She hadn't heard of the actress the girl had mentioned. She realised that she must be from a later series that she had not yet seen. Joanne got to her feet and stumbled across the lobby which was heaving with people. She snuck past a distracted attendee at the doorway to the hotel gym and spa and went into the empty changing rooms. *Everyone must be in the convention*, she realised with a smile. She found a towel hanging on a peg which looked reasonably clean and stepped into the shower. She washed her costume at the same time, making use of the wall soap dispenser in the shower cubicle. Afterwards she wrapped herself in the towel and used a hairdryer station to dry her hair and costume. Feeling refreshed and clean, she nipped back out of the vicinity with the confidence of a paying guest and made her way back to the exhibition hall.

But to Joanne's horror, the TP had gone.

20

Where are you? Joanne spun around, rubbed her eyes, took deep breaths; anything that could wake her up, sober her up or somehow reset the scene in front of her. *This cannot be happening!*

"Hello again!" It was Jason who had appeared beside her. "I'm still shaking. Lucinda was so lovely!" He was flapping a photograph around, evidently in a bid to dry the ink on his freshly signed photo of the glamorous actress. He held out his other hand which was indeed tremoring. Joanne knew the feeling well, having met so many people she had admired. But she struggled to feel his excitement in the current situation. "Are you OK? You look really serious."

"Yeah, I was just ... I was expecting to see a Series 12 TP here this weekend that's all."

"Yeah, there was a TP advertised. But I don't know if it was a Series 12 one and I think they're exhibiting it in the VIP hall or something. I'm not sure why; seems a bit selfish to me. I wouldn't have minded seeing it, but I only have standard tickets. I guess they're using it for exclusive photoshoots with the cast and such."

"Right," said Joanne, trying to piece things together. "Any idea where it is?"

Jason had stopped flapping the picture around and was grinning at it.

"Jason! Do you have any idea where the VIP hall is?"

"No, sorry," he said, without looking up. "Hey, I don't know what plans you have for the day, but do you wanna play cards again later after dinner? A bunch of us are meeting up."

"Er, maybe," she replied, distractedly.

"All right. I guess I'll see you around." He waved cheerily and went off in the direction of one of the merchandise stalls.

Joanne took her phone out of her bag. *Surely there will be a signal in 2022.* But her phone screen was blank and would not turn on and no amount of mashing the home button would help. *I doubt the chargers are the same as 2012. And even if I could get it to work, who would I call?*

Right, first thing's first, she muttered to herself. *I need to find the VIP hall.*

Rosemary was in a quandary. She wanted to spend more time with her mother, but the thought of being stuck in 1994 was at the forefront of her mind. Surely Joanne would come back for her? Even if she went off for a year-long strop, she had a time-machine and could have returned just moments after she had left. She could be in the park now, ready to apologise and make up.

Rosemary asked Emma if she wanted anything from the shop and she declined, which was expected, since her cousin had been for Emma only yesterday. So Rosemary excused herself and left the house, borrowing Emma's winter coat and snow boots. Only instead of going to the shop, she made her way across the road and into the park. The park was empty save for a woman walking a burly Alsatian and two children circling around on bikes on this cool December morning. By the time Rosemary reached the grassy area, the children had cycled out of the gate and the woman was suitably distracted by a struggle against the strength of the dog, which wanted to go in a different direction to its owner. So there was nobody around to notice a booted faerie step into a Christmas tree. She batted the branches and fairy lights out of her path, but to her dismay, the TP was most definitely not there. She closed her eyes, counted to five and opened them again. It was still definitely not there. Rosemary sighed and retraced her steps. She sat down on a bench, startled by the sensation of the frosty wood on her bare legs.

What am I going to do? How long can I effectively wait? she asked herself. *Well, at least Joanne knows where I am. But I have no idea where or when she is. She could be back at ZealCon, back home, somewhere with Jeremy and Alistair, or off on another adventure. What if she's stuck somewhere? What if she's in danger? I'm utterly helpless!* Rosemary thought back to the time they had the encounter with the bandits. Joanne had been brave then. But maybe she had just been lucky. After all, there had been four of them. And now Joanne might be on her own. Just like she was now. A lump formed in her throat and she realised that she was shivering. She stood up and made her way back to the house.

"Did you get anything nice?" Emma asked her, on her return.

"Oh, just a chocolate bar. I ate it on the way back," she lied. Rosemary realised she had lied continually to her mother throughout the entire visit.

"I want chocolate bar!" she heard her younger self say.

"Oh Rosemary, there's plenty of chocolate in the house. It's Christmas after all!"

Rosemary wasn't sure which of them she was talking to for a moment.

"We're going to the cinema later," said her dad, joining them in the lounge. "Would you like to join us, Caroline?"

"What film is it?" Rosemary asked, instantly picturing the Odeon where she had spent many a Saturday afternoon with her dad, even after the tragic event of her mother's death.

"*Miracle on 34th Street,*" he informed her. "It's new."

"Oh, I saw that when it came out," Rosemary blurted, before she could stop herself. Her mum's face fell.

"It's only been out here a couple of weeks. Or was it released earlier in Norway?"

"Or are you talking about the 1947 version?" Her father's geekery was shining out through that serious face of his. "We think this version would be more suitable for little Rosie. She doesn't really get on with black and white films."

Rosemary knew that. She didn't really have the appreciation for classic film until she was a little older. She also knew that she had first seen *Miracle on 34th Street* with her parents in a busy cinema on a cold December day when she was very young ... and she didn't remember anyone else joining them. She also didn't remember anyone else joining them for spaghetti bolognese and ice cream in the pub afterwards either. She specifically remembered what she had eaten that day, because she remembered clambering on the pub's soft play area straight after eating and had got so excitable that her vomit had looked the same coming out as it had going in. She could still see those strings of pasta and pieces of onion smeared down the ball-pool slide now. She could also hear the gasps of horror from the other children and their parents and her own parents apologising profusely to the manager as they whisked her away. It was a vivid memory, with mixed blessings that Rosemary did not wish to taint. She gulped, involuntary. As much as she longed for the little reunion to go on and on, Rosemary knew that it wasn't practical.

"You go. Have fun," she said, looking at each of them one by one. She knelt down and said to the toddler, "And Rosemary, if you go out for dinner afterwards, remember to chew your food properly."

"Hi, can you tell me how I can get access to the VIP area?" Joanne asked once she finally reached the front of the queue at the convention information booth.

"What ticket holder are you?" the portly bearded young man behind the desk asked her. *Why did so many people in*

2022 seem to have beards? she wondered. *And not just small ones, either. Are the men of the world having some kind of competition?* The man glanced at Joanne's lower arm. "You don't appear to have even a standard wrist band." He looked up at her, as though this was new information. He took a swig from an energy drink, gave a not-so surreptitious fruity belch, and awaited her response.

"Er, I lost it," offered Joanne.

"Really?" he asked, not convinced. He consulted a clipboard on his desk. "What's your name? I can get you a new one if we have any spare."

Joanne thought quickly. She looked around the room and at the small queue that was forming behind her. Most people were wearing green wrist bands. One or two were wearing gold ones. *They must be the VIP ticket holders. The girl with the red wig at the gaming table last night had a gold wristband on. What was her name? Come on, Jo, remember!*

"Heidi Furlong," she blurted. She remembered because she had pictured the fictional Swiss girl from the old TV programme saving the world alongside *Terminator 2*'s John Connor when the girl had told her her name and the image had stayed with her.

"Heidi, Hi," said the man with a chuckle and took another swig. "Apologies; I'm an anglophile with a fondness for classic comedy," he said, by way of explanation. He ran his finger down the page, flipped to a second page, then a third page and then stopped. Joanne wondered why everything was not on a computer by now. "Here you are," he confirmed, finally. He put a second tick next to the name and said, "One moment, Heidi." He reached laboriously for a box underneath the desk and pulled out a handful of wristbands. They were all green. He tutted and reached in again, this time retrieving a gold one. He smiled and nodded at Joanne's wrist, which she obediently placed on the desk.

"And don't lose it this time," he warned her with a smile. He obviously enjoyed the feeling of power and responsibility of the position that he held over this short weekend once a year, even if he wasn't the most suitable person for the job. He was far too trusting, for one thing.

She thanked him and then turned to leave. She turned back and asked him for the directions to the VIP area. The disgruntled queue had grown even longer.

"Second floor, third door on your left, ma'am." He gesticulated towards the elevators. Joanne nodded and went on her way. *The second floor in America would be the first floor in England, so that's only one flight*, she reminded herself as she stepped into the lift. She shared the short journey with three other people. She wondered if any of them were famous in 2022 or whether they were attendees, or even imposter attendees like her.

Stepping out onto the next floor, she followed the other three people along the corridor until they reached another queue. *I am fed up of queues. If only I had a time machine.*

21

Once she got to the front of the queue, Joanne could barely suppress her excitement. She ran her fingers over the familiar shape of the Golden Knob and waited for the door attendant to let her through. Flashing her newly acquired wristband, she entered the area which comprised yet more queues. "I'm glad to be at the end of the queue queue," she muttered to herself.

"I know, right?" asked a middle-aged man in cosplay. "What are you going for? A photo-shoot with the Sir Cuthbert cast and the TP, the Doctor and Dalek backdrop or the coffee lounge with *The Big Bang Theory* cast?"

For a moment, Joanne considered doing all three experiences, but she knew she should focus on the task ahead. She wasn't sure what her plan was, but hoped that it would formulate inside her brain by the time she got to the front of the queue. The three VIP encounters were each hidden behind a black curtain, thus hidden from the view of the room and adding to the mystery of the experience.

Joanne voted with her feet and the young man nodded. She realised that he was dressed as a character from *The Big Bang Theory* and joined the coffee lounge queue. He started talking animatedly to the person next to him and Joanne continued to keep herself to herself. The excitement in the room was palpable. Joanne could feel her own excitement rising, too. The plan started to formulate, as she had hoped. Even with the TP behind the curtain, Joanne realised that she couldn't very well put the knob in the lock and make the thing disappear in front of the cast and photographer. She would have to be more subtle than that. She thought back to that first night at ZealCon. Yes, she would get to the front of the queue, check that the TP really was behind the curtain, then she would sneak back later on and make her escape. Her confidence growing, Rosemary reasoned that she might as well even get a cast photograph while she was here.

But things did not go according to plan, for the TP that was revealed behind the curtain was not her TP. It was not even a Series 12 TP. Her face fell.

"What's wrong? Did you join the wrong queue?" asked one the actors, whom she did not recognise. In fact, she didn't recognise any of them. She ran her gaze over the familiar shape of the TP, but it was as though she was seeing it in negative. The material was wrong, the colours were wrong, the whole feel of it was *wrong*.

"It's the wrong TP," she said softly, sadly. "It's not my TP."

"It's the *new* TP!" exclaimed one of the other actors, a woman. "Marvellous, isn't she? It'll be aired in Series – "

"Stop, stop, I don't want to know!" Joanne cried, covering her ears. "I'm, I'm sorry." She threw the curtain aside and fled.

"Hey, Miss, don't you want a picture?" the photographer called after her, but she was already pushing her way back through the queue and out of the room. She ran along the corridor, mindlessly, and came across an alcove with a fridge full of spring water and an ice machine. She pushed a button which dispensed a handful of small cold cubes which she tipped into her mouth and crunched on noisily. It was an odd reaction, but the intense cold hardness seemed to help. Joanne slumped to the floor.

Now what shall I do?

Groups of people walked past her, laughing and joking among themselves. Those not in costume were wearing shorts, slouch jeans or flares. *When did skinny jeans go out of fashion?* Joanne, wondered, ruminating about style being her default thought pattern when stressed. The ice cubes finished, and her mouth numb with cold, she got to her feet and headed back down the corridor, past the VIP area and towards the lifts. Once on the ground floor she battled her way across a busy lobby of queues and yet more queues and went out into the fresh air. Or more accurately, she had to pass through a wall of smoke and vape fumes before she could reach some fresh air. With the chatter of the smokers and vapers behind her, Joanne continued across to the carpark, aimless and lost. A car swerved, out of control, missing her by inches as it rounded a corner. The driver honked the horn and a passenger made a rude gesture out of their open window. Another, in hot pursuit of the first vehicle, zoomed up behind it. Joanne yelped and jumped out of the way. *It's too dangerous here*, she reasoned and sought out the cool shade offered by the side of the hotel. This out-of-the-way area was less grand than the building's frontage and seemed to be home to a large American dumpster, some empty pallets, a team of event staff and … and a *very* recognisable shape.

Rosemary's parents and her younger self had been gone for two hours. During that time she had had a bath, washed and dried her clothes and thought very hard in a bid to figure out a way out of her predicament. She was on her second mince pie when the doorbell rang. Eyes wide, she sprinted along the hallway and tentatively pulled the chain across. In her mind she was her younger self again, left home alone while her parents popped out. Opening the door as far as the chain would allow, she saw a familiar face.

"Jo!" she cried out. Retracting the chain, she opened the door fully and threw her arms around her. She pulled her in close and breathed in her curls. She smelled of shampoo and stale vodka. "I'm so glad you're back! I'm so sorry."

"I'm sorry too!" Joanne had tears in her eyes when they finally drew apart. "Are you ready to come back to the TP?"

"Of course!" Rosemary replied. "I want to stay with my mum, but I've been doing a lot of thinking. I don't belong here, Joanne. Where's the TP?"

"There's a bit of a story about that. I'll tell you on the way. I parked in your tree again."

"*My* tree?" Rosemary said, with a laugh. "Wait a minute. I should write a note. Do we have time?"

"We're time travellers. Of course we do."

"Great." Rosemary gave her friend another quick hug and then reached into a drawer in the telephone table for a pen and paper. The pen was a freebie from her father's work. "I remember these," she said fondly. "I'm just thanking them for their hospitality and telling them that my mum will be in touch. It's a bit of a risk, but it'll have to do."

Joanne nodded and waited while Rosemary left the note and pen on the table and then they both went out into the night. Joanne explained all about escaping to the 2022 convention overnight, how she had unnecessarily got into the VIP area and then eventually located the correct Temporal Perambulator.

"So you found the TP by the rubbish bins?"

"It was being wheeled from the car park to a different entrance. It was being *put up for auction*! So of course I had to hang around all day for the evening prop and memorabilia charity auction because I couldn't get near it without anyone seeing until then. I tried to relax, got a few autographs, hung out in the lobby, chatted with a few people, but I was so scared of not winning the auction. So there we all were, sitting in the main con room, waiting for the auction to start. And they have the usual stuff: signed celebrity pictures and scripts, costumes and such. And then they tell us that there has been an *anonymous donation* of a Series 12 TP. *Our TP!*"

"The cheek of it!! How much did it go for?"

"Hang on a minute, let me talk," Joanne said as they crossed the park once more and headed for the tree. "So everyone's hand shot up when the bidding started at ten dollars, twenty dollars, fifty dollars … after all, this was a *classic* set piece to them in 2022. It was in pretty good nick as far as they were concerned. Anyway, as the number went up and up, fewer and fewer hands stayed up and it went to one thousand dollars, two thousand …"

"*Two thousand?*" Rosemary gasped. Joanne nodded an acknowledgement.

"Three thousand, four thousand …"

Rosemary gasped again.

"Until there was only me and this Mexican guy who must have been retirement age and it got to five thousand five hundred and he *finally* gave in."

"So you won?" asked Rosemary, although she knew she probably already knew the outcome.

"I did, but …"

"But you had the small problem of not having five and a half thousand dollars?"

"Exactly. Well, you know with these things they give you until the end of the convention to pay or whatever, so … I waited until they had put it into a side room and got permission from the auctioneer to nip in to *view it*," she said, using her fingers to make air speech marks. "So while his back was turned I quickly slipped in the Golden Knob, made a swift getaway and here we are!"

"That's some story!"

"I feel terrible. Some children's charity in the future is missing out on five and a half thousand dollars because of me."

"Ah, those children aren't born yet."

"That doesn't really help!"

"Besides," Rosemary reasoned, "you didn't exactly steal anything. *They stole the TP from you.*"

"And we stole it from a con on the other side of the Atlantic in 2012," said Joanne.

"Well, maybe it's time we returned it."

"Before I programme this thing," Joanne said, turning away from the control panel. "I wanted to give you this."

"What is it?"

Joanne held out a piece of paper. "It's your mum's signature. I found it among some stuff while you were writing that note."

"*Among some stuff?*" Rosemary repeated.

"OK, it was at the bottom of a letter on a pile of other letters, addressed to your old pre-school or something. So … it was kind of for you anyway … well … it's *related* to you. But … I didn't suppose you managed to actually ask her for an autograph or anything yourself, so I thought it was er … better than nothing?" Joanne asked, a little embarrassed at her efforts.

"That was a nice gesture. But won't Emma wonder who the hell would rip her signature off the bottom of an official letter – unless they were some kind of fraudster?" She took the scrap of paper from her and placed it between the pages of her autograph book anyway, ready to stick in at a later date.

"Well, that's what I thought too, so I took the rest of the letter as well. In for a penny, and all that." With an awkward smile, Joanne revealed the remainder of the letter and handed it to her. "I just hope it doesn't change anything. For your future, I mean."

Rosemary looked at the letter. "Oh, it's an enquiry letter for Oakham Infant School," she said. "I went to Harringtons Primary and Junior. I heard that Oakham had a bad reputation for bullying – even worse than Harringtons. So you might have actually done me a favour there!" She opened the autograph book again and smiled fondly at her latest acquisition; her ultimate autograph. "Thanks Jo. You're officially forgiven for abandoning me."

Emma Yates

Epilogue

Rosemary had no sooner closed the book than they had landed once more at the Ballington Hotel.

"So, are we returning it before the boys take it?" Rosemary asked, stowing the book.

"Yes. You still want to enjoy the convention, don't you?" asked Joanne, her hand on the door handle.

"But didn't we tell them that we took the TP from *next* year's ZealCon?"

"Quite possibly. A lot has happened since then. I think we've confused them and messed them around enough now. I'm sure we'll see them again."

"I'm pretty sure it's destiny," said Rosemary with a shriek.

"Ah yes. The whole marriage thing. And we didn't even get their numbers."

"I wonder if we'll ever find out how the TP works," said Rosemary.

"It's been bothering you, hasn't it?"

"Hasn't it been bothering you?"

"Our future selves seems rather smug. I'm sure we find out eventually."

"Perhaps, Jo. Perhaps."

Stepping out of the TP and into the exhibition hall, they traipsed across the carpet, its iconic geometric pattern just visible as the TP's engine cooled and its lights flickered out.

"Oh, I should return this," said Joanne, holding up the Golden Knob. Alistair and Jeremy will have trouble taking it without that."

"And I suppose you and I should keep in touch too. Not just yearly at this hotel. I mean, if we're to become hot-shot screen writers and all."

"No pressure," Joanne sighed, suddenly feeling overwhelmed at the idea of it all.

"No pressure."

"What do you want to do now? Sleep? Bar?"

"I'm too wired to sleep. And I think my socialising meter is full for now."

"Oh, so you want to be alone?" asked Rosemary. Her shoulders dropped.

"Nah. I came to ZealCon to meet you and the rest of the Faerie Gathering, didn't I? Want to pore over some faerie folklore books in our room in preparation for tomorrow?"

"Never did something so simple sound so appealing. Let's go and study those books."

"You big geek."

"Always."

The End.

Or, if you haven't read The Extreme Autograph Hunters, read that one next as it runs parallel with this story.

ALSO BY RUTH MASTERS

THE TRUXXE TRILOGY

Three novels following the adventures of Tom Bowler, a human who finds himself working in an intergalactic service station during his gap year. He discovers the secrets of the planetoid Truxxe, traverses the galaxy to rescue his alien friend from the prison planet Porriduum and ultimately defends the earth against an alien invasion.

A cast of colourful aliens good and bad, fantastic alien worlds and witty dialogue make this trilogy a great read for any sci-fi fan!

Vol 1: All Aliens Like Burgers
Vol 2: Do Aliens Read Sci-Fi?
Vol 3. When Aliens Play Trumps

AUTOGRAPH HUNTER SERIES

A pair of "paraquels", each covering similar events, from the perspective of different characters. In both books, attendees at the same sci-fi convention happen across a real working time machine, and set off on autograph-hunting missions through time.

The two pairs of friends cross paths occasionally, with Rosemary and Joanne intriguingly being one step ahead of Alistair and Jeremy. Along the way they meet the great and the good of history, from Shakespeare to the inventor of the modern toilet. Friendships are tested and life will never be the same again…

Vol 1: Extreme Autograph Hunters
Vol 2: Ultimate Autograph Hunters

BELISHA BEACON & TABITHA TURNER

Tabitha Turner is a complaints executive from contemporary Birmingham. Belisha Beacon is a celebrity DJ working on the illustrious Möbius Strip, orbiting the planet Hayfen IV, 400 years in the future.

Inexplicably finding themselves inhabiting each other's bodies and living each other's lives the two women must survive in a strange new world.

How will they get back to their own realities… and do they want to? Nothing is ever as it seems as Belisha and Tabitha's lives begin to change forever.

Order from www.ruthmastersscifi.com or on Amazon.